# Nothing
# Lasting

# Nothing Lasting

LAURA SOLOMON

Published by Woven Words Publishers OPC Pvt. Ltd., 2018
**Branch Office(Operational)**: H. No. 8-1-346/19/A/1 & 2, Flat no. 504, 5th Floor, Zara Residency, Brindavan Colony, Toli Chowki, Hyderabad 500 008, Telangana.

www.wovenwordspublishers.com
Copyright© Laura Solomon, 2018

ISBN-13: 978-93-86897-38-1

ISBN-10: 93-86897-38-5


Price: $25/₹250

Printed and bound in India

He is my host he is my guest
He gave his worst he took my best
The blessing will remain a curse
Till servant master is reversed
And when the final race is run
The battle lost is the battle won.

We all have hearts and we all have minds.

-Anon

# Contents

# EPISODE ONE

## *In The Beginning*

My old man used to say, if you play with fire, then you're gonna get burnt. That's just shite. You only get burnt if you're thick. If you've got two cerebral cells to knock together, you light the match and you run, like it's not the building that's on fire, but your own dumb self. You don't sit around waiting for the engines and the sirens and the onlookers, your feet just hit that pavement and you move so fast that you don't even have time to look down and notice the cracks that you're landing on. And should you choose to pause, and look back over your shoulder, there wouldn't be nothing, as far as the eye could see, but orange light and blazing flame and the building on the far horizon falling.

And the city behind you, dissolving into light.

## *First Burning*

I was once addicted to arson. You might find this strange coming from a nice guy like me, but it's true.

*It was boredom and the devil made me do it.*

In the two years leading up to that first lighting I had not done a hell of a lot with my life. Not a lot constructive as they say, though I was never quite sure what it was that I was meant to be constructing. Model boats or aeroplanes, perhaps, but I never had been too keen on working with my hands. I never had been too keen on a lot of things: my town, my family, my friends, girls, my country, animals, God. I had not been too keen on anything really, but once I discovered fire, I was dead sold on that.

*What I want to tell you about is how it all began and how I could never be sure whether I was sliding or on the ascent or whether it was the same thing anyway.*

My compulsion was both heaven and hell. First came the desire for release and destruction, then the burst of flame which seemed to me to come from elsewhere and reach to elsewhere. Only afterwards, usually at night, did my emptiness and guilt return from the place to which they had been driven by the force of the flame. And then I would banish these feelings again, with the planning of the next day's pyromaniac activities. Don't misunderstand me. I don't feel proud of the destruction I wreaked upon the country. I feel very ashamed. I am only trying to make you understand why I did what I did. The desire for loss of control, for oblivion, was the same in each case. And, of course, after each crime committed, I was left emptier than before, and sought relief in even greater destruction.

*But I never meant to hurt anybody, I swear it.*

And all that time, the terrible longing, the terrible hunger which consumed both my mind and my soul, as if it was I that was on fire, and not that which I lit. The more I destroyed, the more I wanted to destroy, and there seemed to me no way to break the vicious cycle into which I had become locked. Nor did I wish to disrupt this pattern. The consequences of my actions were not important to me; no, they did not matter one single bit. As long as I was left alone by the authorities, I was happy to continue wreaking havoc. Of course, I felt the guilt and the shame of having done what might be seen as morally and lawfully "wrong" and yet every bone in my body sang out that what I was doing was right.

*I never intended to commit any crime, please believe me.*

I was just a nice normal middle-classer. One thing led to another and the next thing you know...

I gave up the grip on myself so easily. It was as if all I had been holding onto was the string of a helium filled balloon and, once I had let go, I found myself drifting into pleasant and weightless areas of compulsion.

*It was not anything much, the first thing I lit, it was just a little farmhouse.*

But it signified what you might call the beginning of the end.

*They'd even left all the lights on.*

I gave the place a liberal dousing of kerosene, struck my match and got the hell out of there.

Burnt like a forest in midsummer. As the first flames licked the sky, her wires began to spark, and she shot out fireworks in every direction. Talk about a sight for sore eyes.

*Then I saw something like hair on fire, then I saw something like a body on fire, and then I saw him, bashing on the upstairs pane, pure terror in his eyes.*

He burnt right in front of me, and I felt sicker than I ever had in my life. Nausea swept over me; I felt the first stabs of a migraine and began to shake. The figure's banging became more and more frantic, reached a climax, and then began to slow until he collapsed out of sight behind the sash of the window. I felt myself collapse also, and lay on the ground, chest heaving, sick with horror at what I had done. I had burned with him.

I don't know how I found my way home that night. Certainly, there seemed to be no roads anywhere, or if there were, then they looped back on themselves, circular. But I awoke in the night, back in my room, the old four walls signifying arrival. And I saw before my vision, time and again, the horrified face of my victim. The walls began to twist and distort, as if I were not in a room at all, but tossing on a violent ocean, with no land in sight.

*O where was my pacific paradise now?*

Breaker crashed in upon breaker, my heart sang violence, violence and more violence, yet the thought of the face at the window made me rile against this initial lust for action. My thoughts were divided into two opposing teams; on the one hand, impulse, who would have me burn whole villages, towns and cities, and on the other hand, repulsion, who made me sick at the thought of the death that impulse had instigated. Torn between these two armies, I was as helpless as a lamb. How could I be my own good shepherd?

Now the way out was really barred, the door locked from the outside, and every window boarded over with plain white planks. I fondled my kerosene tin lovingly. Here it was, my arsenal, my weaponry, my sweet loaded gun.

*They say that fire makes a good servant but a bad master.*

I must refuse to serve.

I doused myself, and struck the match.

# EPISODE TWO

*Bleach*

It didn't work. Somebody 'up there' had decided that I was not to be given the mercy of quick death, and so I came back to myself. The first thing I saw when I opened my eyes was a red quivering mass making its way towards my lips. Thinking this to be my heart, or some other internal organ, I began to struggle, spitting and screaming and yelling. It struck me briefly that I may have been captured by some primitive tribe (or, more likely, a local gang) and that it may be these people who were now force feeding me my own vitals.

A yell went out.

"Shona! Get the lime! He don't like this Raspberry!", and my eyes readjusted themselves to take in a mountainous bosom and a jelly-laden spoon.

"Momma?", I muttered softly, questioningly.

Footsteps pattered into the room.

"Quick Shona, get some of that down his throat, or we'll lose him again."

A spoonful of lime jelly headed my way, and I took it down, gratefully, like a baby.

God! How had I come to this!

"He's lucky to be alive, this one."

How lucky I did not feel! I tried to raise my right arm to brush away a fleck of jelly I could feel on the side of my cheek. Nothing moved. I made an attempt with the left arm; still nothing moved. I gave a small cry of frustration. The face of the nurse who was not Shona started coming into focus, slowly, as if a camera were being adjusted.

Her slab of a face hung in the air like a cardboard cut-out moon; a raw lump of dough slammed down on a rolling board, white scone mix. Scone-dough's face was framed by a mass of brown fuzz, the hairs so thick and wiry, they seemed pubic. Repulsion rose within me.

Shona was marginally more attractive. At least, she had a colour combination I admired - red hair and green eyes. The rest was a mass of white. I looked down and saw that this white was my own body; head to toe in bandages.

"Second and third degree", said Shona, "you'll be needing a lot of surgery."

"You'll also be taking part in our psychiatric program", said Sconeface, with a wolverine grin. "Voluntarily", she added as an afterthought.

So I was here, stuck, in the State Hospital with the reek of ammonia and the cotton wool claustrophobia. Bandages covered every part of me, but for my eyes, mouth and nostrils. There was a hole cut at the end of the bandage which covered my penis, so that I could urinate, and another sliced near my anus so I could defecate. I was reduced to an animal, less than an animal, a robot, an automaton. I was inertia incarnate. I cannot even begin to describe the intensity of the boredom I experienced. Seconds seemed to take minutes, minutes seemed to take hours, hours took days, and days took an eternity to pass. Of course, the other patients could while away the time with cards or bridge or scrabble, but I was sentenced to lie hour after hour, flat on my back. Once a day, at approximately ten o'clock, Shona and Sconeface would came and hoist me onto my feet, and there I would totter, supported only by these two custodians for a minute or two, before I was lowered back onto the bed. That was the day's exercise.

Inside my bandages, I was rotting, mummified. At least I knew my own release date. I was to be confined to my bed for two weeks, and then the bandages could be removed. I was not to look in a mirror until after the plastic surgery, lest the shock knock me cold. It was the doctor who had told me this; a cold-faced, cold-hearted, surgical sort of a man with a nervous disposition. His only duty towards me seemed to be to act as messenger of bad news regarding my second-rate third-degree burns; the rest of the duties were carried out by the nurses. They fed me. Cornflakes, FruitLoops, Two Minute Noodles, Maggi Creme of Chicken soup, Edmond's jelly. Nourishing sustenance blurred into nourishing sustenance. All I could think of was the two week release date - my lighthouse beacon of hope in an ocean of emptiness.

Shona and Scone delighted in bringing faces cut out from magazines. They would press these upon me, certain that now I had obliterated my own face, I would be free to create a new one. I could chose from a range of male fashion models, famous actors, rock stars.

"Of course we couldn't do you exactly like Richard Gere, you haven't got the bone structure for it, but we could do you over in the likeness of Richard, a sort of slightly smudged carbon copy."

I had no desire to be good looking. My profession dictated invisibility. I must possess the kind of looks which would neither attract nor repulse. I must wear the face of nobody.

I must admit to feeling a slight attraction towards Shona during this period of my life. Of course, it was only a case of a droplet of water appearing to be a refreshing mountain stream when one is stranded in the desert, but she was kind, good-natured, and most importantly, young. I estimated her to be in her late twenties or early thirties, whereas Scone was not a day under fifty-five. It was a little hard to flirt in full-body bandages. Still, I managed the odd suggestive comment, and old Shona played right along with it. I figured that once I was a famous arsonist she would fall into my arms as easily as a skydiver with a failed chute, although hopefully she would not be quite as heavy. So I filled my days with daydreaming about being made over with the face of nobody, becoming a successful arsonist and winning Shona into my life. The two of us could light little fires together; two phoenixes. Like they say, dreaming is free. It's the nightmares you have to pay for.

I saw nothing of the other patients, and they saw nothing of me. Shona and Scone were my only company, and being as they were with me for only twenty minutes at a time, three times a day, I spent most of my hours thinking. Thinking is a terrible occupation. Horrid visions of the face at the window pane would come to haunt me, and time and time again, I would wish that the neighbours had not found me. For it was they who had turned the fire extinguisher onto my singed body, and saved the life I hadn't wanted to save; my own. How had I not noticed that there had been somebody home at the farmhouse? Failure weighed in upon me. Despite my morbid thoughts, I knew that I hadn't been brought back from the dead for nothing. I had a duty and a calling. I would target only those in that parasitic group who undermine the very fabric that our society is made of; the wealthy. Now only the select would become my victims and to be my victim would be a privilege. Why should some poor farmhand die to indulge me? I would not only be an arsonist, I would also be a killer. But I would isolate and kill only those who deserved to die. It was my sense of a mission that brought me through my dark days; those savage two weeks that led up to my surgical reconstruction.

Of course, the day eventually came, like all days eventually do. The doctor came in and twitched nervously and removed my body bandages. The skin underneath was wrinkled and pink, like that of a new-born baby mouse. I felt cleansed, as if my past life were being peeled away with the old dead skin. I had thought that my face would be like this, also; new-born. But when the facial bandages were peeled, I was still forbidden to see my face. But you know the next bit. I need not tell you that the first thing I did was hunt out a mirror in order to peek at what I thought would be my new baby-soft face. On my unsteady limbs, I made my shaky way down the corridor to the bathroom. No baby-face this. I looked upon death itself. My facial tissue was charcoaled, barbequed, a delicacy.

The mirror smashed and I must have had some sort of a fainting fit. The world turned upside down. Silver blurred on liquid silver; the mirror which had contained me shimmered like water, and I felt myself begin to slide away. All I had believed was solid fell apart, the silver dripped down and I found that I had gone through the wall, or through the mirror which I had hitherto believed was palpable. I was unable to discern whether this land I now inhabited was real and all else the reflection, or whether my previous life on the 'right' side of the mirror had been the real thing and all that now surrounded me was reflection, in which case, I was now, also, only a reflection.

I was completely alone, and all was silence but for a consistent plinking as the mirror continued its slow dissolution. At my feet was a pool where the glass had melted. If I tried to look back at where I had been, I could see nothing, and feared, in looking, that I too would become like Lot's wife as she had fled the burning city. So it was that I turned my mind to its new environment; not out of choice, but by force. For I had not chosen to come here, but had stumbled, or fallen, or had a kind of fainting fit, and found myself suddenly through the glass. It was as if my reflection had tired of being a reflection, and had decided that it would be quite nice to have a life of its own. When I say that I could see nothing, that's exactly what I mean. Nothing surrounded me. All was completely white, as if it had been snowing seagull feathers or plain white rice. Indeed, the landscape and the heavens had both had been given such a decent bleaching that it was impossible to tell where land became sky and sky became land, or even which was which. All that indicated which way was up, was gravity. At first, by looking down at my feet, I could understand the concept of terra firma. Then it struck me that not only had I gone through the mirror, but that my world had also turned upside down, and that I was actually standing on the sky. This ought to have shaken me, and indeed I began to feel terror's tight hand close in around my skull. However, I reasoned, I must have come here for something I had wanted, for something long lost or long forgotten, and so, I ceased to be afraid, and drew courage from my weakness. The more I trembled, the stronger I felt. It struck me that I might have mistakenly lurched my clumsy way into some Northern King's Ice Palace of Paradox's.

I remembered, in snatches, parts of my previous life spent on the 'right' side of the mirror. All I could recall was that I had once walked as a profession; walked and walked and walked, for hours on end, right around the town, often looping back upon my own track, passing the same cafe and library and museum time and time again. Often things had passed me by in a haze of rain and umbrellas. The trick is to always look as if you are headed somewhere, so as to avoid suspicion. Of course, the truth is that you are headed nowhere. This technique of nowhere walking is known to all those who slip through cracks and wrinkles in the fabric of society; the homeless, the jobless, the elderly, the alcoholic, the chronically melancholic, the criminal. All such people practise this dubious skill; it is a way of life, a sampling of non-existence, as if by being nowhere definite, one might cease to be anywhere at all. Perhaps I had spent some time at an art gallery admiring the sepia-tinted photographs upon the walls, or perhaps I had sat at a bus-stop, acting as if there were somewhere I had to be at some particular time, shuffling my feet impatiently and looking anxiously down the road at a bus that I knew would never come. I had wished for nowhere, and the Good Fairy had smiled upon me with her magic wand; all my dreams had come true. I could not remember my time at the hospital, nor could I remember my acts of arson; all pain had been erased from my memory. All I could remember was wishing for nothing. And now I had found it.

For here I was in the trackless wilderness of the bleached sky, hopelessly disorientated. Now that the mirror had completely dissolved there was no sound whatsoever, not even so much as the chirping of a cricket's horn. Where the mirror had stood, now there was a doorway, solid oak, ornately carved. It was the only obstacle which broke the white perfection; yet I was glad to see it, it was a relief, like a relief ornament, meant to break the harshness of no sight. It broke the monotony like the sonic boom of an aeroplane. It boldly stated its own existence; it stood.

Moving up to the frame, I grasped each side firmly with my hands and peered through. Like the bear who went over the mountain, all that I could see was the other side of the snow. Yet I was petrified to leave my frame, now that it had materialised, for it was a thing tangible in a world where all else shifted like liquid. Still I could not forget that this was a world which obeyed no laws, and just as the door had appeared, so too might it vanish, and I would be left, wrecked, solitary. Though now the door seemed not to stand, but float. Everything was awash; a vast white fishless ocean - no longer had I stumbled into nothing - now I was the proverbial sailor with a doorframe for a life raft. Of course I thought, as you would think, that this was my way out, my salvation. It occurred to me the door may be a cliff of hell cleverly disguised, for who could know what a door would really signify if it were only a reflection? Still, I took my punt, as you, or your neighbour, or your neighbour's cousin would take his or her punt; though not much of a gamble considering the alternatives. I stepped through the doorway, and found myself, not back in my room, but rather, in somebody else's dining room.

The table was set, as if the host were giving a great banquet. The plates were gilt-edged, and the glasses crystal. The knives and forks were solid silver and in the centre of the table sat a large basted turkey surrounded by baked apples. My stomach clenched itself into a tight fist as I felt nausea rise within me at the richness of the food. What I really longed for now was not some fancy banquet but some plain spuds and mash, perhaps a few frozen peas. The banqueting room made me homesick for the home I had never known. Host and guests were absent; all was suspended, waiting for the arrivals. A far-off rustling was heard, and the diners entered, all splendidly arrayed in moroon and gold robes, but for the host, who appeared cloaked in black. I waved frantically, yet nobody seemed to see me, and I felt myself slipping away again, smaller and smaller; a shadow on the wall. The fourteen diners seated themselves at the table; still nobody spoke a word. I felt at once petrified that I would be seen, yet also hopeful that somebody would notice me and cancel my suspicions that I had ceased to exist. For I felt myself to be nothing, or less than nothing, and knew that without disguise or costume I did not exist; for only in dressing up could I take any form. I was the shadow that made the mask move and that was about it. The advantage was that I had been given the power to "make myself up" as I wished; just as easily could I dissemble myself - just as easily could everything fall away to leave me cast in the outer regions of Abyssinia. For I was sure now, that I had been in Abyssinia's mirrored reflection - the hottest of climates when inversed by the mirror could only become the most polar of all polar regions.

Still I was unable to discern my present whereabouts. The diners had begun to eat - all with the most regal of table manners. They seemed to share some secret, which made talk unnecessary - though whether they thought speech was beneath or above them, I did not know. I felt myself to be an invisible sacrifice - ignored until such a time as they would butcher and eat me; for there was something both carnivorous and carnivalesque about the scene. Perhaps I was the sacrificial lamb - I would be strung on the altar. I had slipped both backwards and forwards in time, or else, into eternity. Still, nobody had acknowledged my presence. I was only present as an absence.

Then this scene also began to melt. The great thaw had begun. A crack in the ice, a great divide opened up beneath my feet and I stood astride a vast abyss. The diners also began to drift away from me. I lost my footing and began to plunge, only to find that I was not falling at all, but was coming up through the anaesthetic, as a deep-sea diver surfaces.

I had been under "the knife", as they put it. Shona had found me collapsed on the bathroom floor, the sight of myself having made me pass out, or pass away into my own personal Siberia. There had been a space, apparently, where I had come to my senses and begged for surgery, something non-descript, a face that would blend into any crowd. So they had put me under, re-made me and I had come up kicking. Scone held a mirror up to my face, and I saw that no longer was my facial tissue charcoaled.

My reconstructed mug bore the mocking grin of nobody.

# EPISODE THREE

## *Home*

I returned home a new man.  My last day in the hospital had seen me falling flat on my face Shone-wise; asking for a date, and being refused outright.
None of the "I'll be washing my hair, taking the dog for a walk, watering the potplants".  Just a flat, simple "I think you're pretty fucked in the head mate - plus, I don't go for men with who've blistered."  Of course, I didn't really mind this rejection.  I took it pretty well.  I simply swore to dedicate myself more completely to my cause.  Somewhere along the way, the fear had turned to fight.  Not for nothing had I been brought back from the dead.  The rich would burn in their beds.  I divided my life into four easy segments; compartments within which to contain the chaos that yapped at my heels.  The Weather, Home, The Disguise and the Future.

### *The Weather Report.*

While nothing had moved at the hospital, time had really flown by back here at home.  What had been autumn had bleached itself into the winter months; a strange mockery of my anaesthetic mirror world.  Lolly coloured leaves no longer fell, wind no longer roared down from the heavens; all was white, silent and still.  Wiping the pane, I could see blankness stretching out eternally; a white blanket covering houses, gardens, automobiles, lampposts.  A landscape begging for a burning.  Fire in the snow and all that shite.

### *My Home Town  - Shackleton.*

Finding the wealthy would be a piece of piss.  Like all towns, mine was separated into divisions according to income.  I rented in the "scunge" division; rotting weatherboards, graffitied walls, charred back fences.  I was down near the railway and the sea, among the warehouses, the electrical suppliers, the drowning businesses and the bus stations. On the other side of the shops, away from the sea, but still on the flats, were those in the middle income bracket. The retailers, the school teachers, the sales clerks. And above the sea, on "The Heights" which rose towering above the town, were those in the upper divisions of wealth. The real earners – who had once been nerdy kids that were bullied at school; the doctors, the pilots, the lawyers, the computer programmers, the company managers. Shackleton existed in the no-man's land between a city and a town. The neuroses of small town life mingled with the class and wealth divisions of a city to produce a mutant offspring; an abortion, a clown of a city, a retard of a town. A good burn would do Shackleton a world of good.

*The Disguise.*

In the snow, the best disguise would prove to be white. No longer did I need to wear a face mask - my face was a mask. Still, the body must be cloaked. I was the proud owner of a yellow stretch jumpsuit - with a little soaking in bleach, this would do just fine. I, myself, would be indistinguishable from the snow. I would work only at night; a phantom shape slithering across the frosty landscape - a rattlesnake, striking and recoiling, striking and recoiling.

*The Future, The Night, Infinite Hope.*

Going to bed that night, I was bursting with hope for my future. Fame, Immortality, Mansonesque noteriety. The names of my victims would be writ large in flame. Only the privileged would die by my hand. I constructed a short mantra; douse with the left, light with the right, douse with the left, light with the right. Sleep drifted in, carrying me away on the endless ocean of a sentence.

I awoke to the cheerful rustling of the rats which chewed at the pink bats insulating the walls of the flat. The first thing to check on would be my bleached jumpsuit. It lay in its liquid, a few tattered strands, having been almost completely devoured by the bleach. It seemed as if everything was being consumed. Yet, the threads hung together in the rough semblance of a costume. Gaps in the stomach and buttock areas, but a decent covering in the groin and chest regions. If I stayed away from the sunbed, I should blend into my surroundings like a true chameleon. How proud my parents would be when they saw my remodelled face on the evening news. How they would turn to each other and cry "Our blessed son! We always knew life held great things for him!" And if I did return home, they would embrace me lovingly, perhaps cook up a bit of a mixed grill and we would play happy families with the best of them. Shona would be left, an anaemic ghost, endlessly wandering the hospital corridors, muttering about what could have been....if only......if only! If only was about to become action.

***

Loris Knight had been in all my classes at high school. She was the much-loved daughter of Doris and Horace Knight; a couple of successful entrepreneurs who ran a lucrative chain of jewellery stores imaginatively entitled "Knight Jewellers". Our school was 'streamed' so all us 'accelerated' kids were shoved together into one class where the majority of us proceeded to define the term "little shit". We had to prove ourselves to the rest of the school - prove that we were just as capable of making the teacher cry, smoking at lunchtime, pashing by the bike sheds. At least it was up to everybody else to live these dramas. I didn't live, I watched. This was my function. I was always on the outside looking in. And I watched nobody more than I watched Loris. Loris *was* popularity. She had everything; the best clothes, the coolest music, the roundest breasts, the blackest mascara. Everything she touched just turned to gold.

Both teachers and students adored her - a feat previously considered unattainable. Not only did she excel both academically and on the sports field, but as she wandered the schoolyard she was greeted with cries of "Hey Loris! Coming for a milkshake!", "Loris, come shoot some baskets" and the most infamous "Hey! My friend likes you!" And she handled it all with graceful aplomb. Loris haunted me through high school. She was class president in the third form, Captain of the basketball team and high jump champion in the Fourth Form, prefect and top in English, Maths, Chemistry and Biology in the sixth form, Dux and Head of the Ball Committee in the Seventh Form.

O dear God how I hated Loris Knight. I came to think of her as my nemesis; for every success of hers, I experienced several intense failures. Crippling myself with a shot-put, coming bottom of physics, maths and Japanese. Tuning out the cries of "Take a shower" or "Faggot!" which pursued me as I stalked my solitary way across the school field, always walking rapidly, as if I had some place to go to, when really I had no destination and nobody to go there with. I would walk past Loris and her solid core of friends and fantasize that we had, somehow, magically, changed places, so that it was now I who was surrounded by a group of cooing friends, and being asked to go "shoot a few baskets".

No-one deserved to burn more than Loris.

The Knights owned an expansive property up on "The Heights". The rumour about town was that they'd just spent twenty thousand dollars on new shag-pile carpet. Most of the houses in Shackleton were surrounded by fences and trees - not the Knight's. Their lawn was "walk on" and extended for a whole acre and a half. This expanse of green was kept neatly mown at all times. Loris' bedroom was at the front of the house - she looked out over the whole of Shackleton like a princess. When she came home from university that was. She'd gotten straight into second year med, had our Loris, breezed on in there with that ninety per cent average. The thought of Loris treating pus-ridden boils and old hypochondriac alcoholics made me momentarily joyful - then it struck me that she'd probably go into some overpaid, prestigious branch of medicine. Psychiatry, paediatrics, chiropody.

If I couldn't burn Loris, I could burn her room.

Please don't think me misogynist. It wasn't Loris' gender that made me want to commit this act. It was her status in the community; a pillar of all I wanted for myself, yet hated because I couldn't have. When I look back now, at this twisted stage of my life, I can see that my mind was playing tricks on itself. Shadows falling upon shadows, mirrors reflecting darkness upon other mirrors - and myself a crumpled marionette, the strings jerked by an idiotic and tyrannical master. What I needed to burn was not some outside enemy, but the enemy within myself. And yet the master had such a grip on me that he could convince me to destroy only what lay outside of myself, and not the enemy that lay within. I was a soldier,

24

confused by the war. In my hands had been placed a loaded gun; yet I was impotent to fight. I had no bullets, only blanks.

So it was that I found myself, that fateful night, outside Loris' bedroom, kerosene can in one hand, match in the other. History was about to happen. I could feel time pulsing through my veins; clotted blood; choked arteries - all had been leading to this one moment - moving inwards, into the eye of the storm, the hurricane bursting, my moment of release. I stood, tighter than a magnet's coil. Wound, fit, ready to kill, a panther primed for action. All hung, suspended for this one moment. I teetered on the brink of 'I-knew-not-what". All I knew, all knowledge, was the edge I stood on; all abyss stretched its empty arms before me. The master snapped his whip. I fell back into the past.

On my eighteenth birthday, my mother was committed to Shackleton State Hospital. My father and I each took an arm, and led her gently to the car, murmuring bribes and condolances. "You'll have raspberry jelly every night", "we've packed your favourite pink nightie", "the best in the country". We handed my mother over to the head nurse, and we went home and shared the cake she had been baking the night before. It was a sponge, cut in the shape of the numbers "1" and "8", covered in pink icing upon which were ornate flowers; lilies, tulips, pansies. My father ate the "1" while I successfully devoured the "8". We told each other that we had done the right thing, that it would only be temporary, that we couldn't manage Mother any longer. We carried on as a normal-family-minus-the-mother. I was in the seventh form; my father was working for an electrical supplier.

My mother had always been a model of femininity. She had done all it took to be a woman; bleached her hair since age fourteen, sung with a group of girls called the "Shangrilas", ironed and starched collars, cleaned out dirty pantries, thrown dinner parties, washed menstrual stains from underwear and raised a baby boy (your humble narrator). At age thirty-nine, something in the model snapped. I would come home from school, alone, to find my mother sitting in front of the television, huddled beneath a stack of blankets, smoking Pall Mall reds and cursing. She started swearing at my father. "You stupid asshole, I should have married somebody with brains! An electrician! What's going to happen to you? Do you know what's going to happen to you? You're going to get old and die, that's what. And nobody will remember you, nobody will remember who fixed the problem in their wires! A waste, that's what you lifetime's been, a waste!" Of course, the problem was not with my father's wasted life, but with my mother's. The darkness in her mind cast shadows upon the outside world until all was blackened in a boundless night. My father was a hopeless moron. I was the evil son, a curse sent from above. Things declined. The moment the television was switched off, my mother would begin yelling. My failure, my father's failure, the failure of the family in the face of the world. The critic sang. My mother sat as Judge and Jury on anything we did. The family doctor was called in for help. He diagnosed Lithium, Prozac, Valium, anything to shut my mother up, to close her mouth with Superglue. And when none of the above worked, we had to take her to the hospital. The problem was, nobody knew what it was she needed or wanted. She seemed insatiable; insufferable. In her eyes, the world was filled with lunatics, yet she herself was sane. All the world was in despair; yet she herself played host to ecstasy. My father and I were failures; her life defined success.

On the night before my eighteenth birthday my father and I had recorded that my mother had spent the last twenty-three days in the same nightgown. I had come home from birthday-eve to find that she had started to bake my cake. I told her she didn't have to; I would have been perfectly content with an Earnest Adams mandarin and chocolate sponge with false cream filling. Yet still she baked. I sat at the kitchen table, watching her move, wishing that I was somewhere else; that I was somebody else. I transported myself into the Knight family kitchen. I didn't just imagine Loris; I was Loris. My two younger twin brothers sat across the table from me, ladling gravy onto their chicken. Mum and Dad joked happily in the kitchen; Dad carving up some more meat, Mum taking the potatoes out of the oven with a happy grin. And there I was; beauty queen material, brain of bloody Britain, the phone ringing every five minutes, "Loris, it's for you!", "Could somebody please take the phone off the hook over dinner, so we could have some peace. Loris, you'll have to tell your friends not to call until after eight o'clock." The brothers squabbling amicably, myself playing elder

26

sister, "Quiet kids!"......I came crashing back to reality; my mother was breaking eggs on her scalp and sliding them into the bowl, whisking the yokes and whites with her fingers, and adding a chunk of spit to water down the mix. We had done all we could to help; it was time to take her to the professionals.

It was the divide between Loris' world and my own that was the fuel to the flame. My act of burning would be an act of justice; I would not be burning Knights' family home, but all that Loris stood for. Beauty, poise, elegance, athleticism, grace. I was burning on behalf of all that I represented - ugliness, clumsiness, sloth and gracelessness. I thought of my mother spitting into my eighteenth birthday cake and drew new courage. Through my fragmented mind raced images of the face at the farmhouse window, of Shona's face, of the guests and the banquet, of my mother cracking eggs. I threw kerosene onto the wood beneath Loris' bedroom window, struck the match and watched the blaze. I ran, then, as if my own fire were pursuing me.

# EPISODE FOUR

*Elsewhere*

It didn't fuck up.  Success.  My absence was plastered over the front page of the local rag the next morning.  An imaginative headline - "Arsonist at Work in Shackleton".  And a nice little article - "Police are currently trying to discern the whereabouts and identity of a pyromaniac seen fleeing from the site of last night's torching.  The Knight family watched in horror as their beautiful family home collapsed before their very eyes.  The man is considered to be dangerous and psychologists say that he is likely to strike again."  Strike.  That was good.  They'd got the snake thing.
"The arsonist was seen sprinting from the scene of the crime.  The man was unmasked."  Unfortunately, they hadn't picked up on the "K" that blazed on the front lawn.  I had been attempting to write "Knight", (the names of my victims in flame) when the fire engines and the police came hurtling round the corner.  But this was to be my trademark, my sign, my mark and they had missed it.  Pack of ignoramuses.  The article went on.  "Fortunately, nobody was injured in the fire."  I exhaled softly.  My feelings regarding this were mixed.  On the one hand, death or injury would have attracted more attention to the deed.  On the other - the mental movie screen played time and time again the live footage taken on the night of my first major arson at the farmhouse.  The man screaming and burning upstairs, bashing against the pane, sparking and crackling.  Bile rose in my throat.

The picture beneath the report showed a dressing-gowned Doris and Jeremy outside the family home, the two younger twin brothers clutched anxiously in front of them.  Loris' absence was not mentioned.  Guilt rose, but was kept down with the thought of my mother at the kitchen sink cracking eggs upon her scalp.  Of course!  I was not avenging myself, but my family.  I was crossing the divide between my own world of poverty, solitude and misery and Loris' world of wealth, popularity and joy.  In burning Loris' home, something of Loris would rub off on me - the fire would work

28

magical charms. From wearing the face of nobody, would come the ability to be somebody else. I would absorb Loris into me and become a Knight.

At home, the following day, my plans expanded. Success fed ambition. Shackleton just wasn't enough to satisfy my appetite for flame. I would have to seek fulfilment elsewhere. The closest major city was Enderby, with a population somewhere between three and four hundred thousand. Perfect for anonymity. A boy could become pleasantly lost in a place like that. Live quietly in a bedsit, perhaps take some casual work driving taxis.....It was also time that I hot-footed it out of Shackleton. Twenty-four years in a place like that was twenty-four years too many. Five years through toddlerhood, fourteen years of schooling, two years living at home on the dole, two years living away from home on the dole - my career meant that I could leave all that behind me. I felt myself travelling away from my past at the speed a rocket ascends from the earth. All trauma had existed in another life; had happened to another person. Now that I was nobody, I could move to another city and really be somebody. Looking back, that was all I had ever wanted. Looking back was not a good idea. The thought of my past made me nauseous, dizzy, vertiginous. Better to imagine my new life into existence, to concentrate on making the impossible possible.

I suppose you'll be wondering about my folks. Like I said, I only wanted to make them proud of their little boy. I only ever wanted to do right by them. With the money from magazine interviews, I could get my mother some fantastic new medication, my father would be as proud as that fateful day the first fifteen was announced. They could buy a flashy little apartment in town; sell off their rundown shack. I could buy mother's mental health.

She had stayed at Shackleton State Hospital for three months, during which time my father and I lived off baked beans, two-minute noodles, microwave pizzas and beer. We would visit her in the green and white sterility of the ward. All that she did was stand. Upon arrival, she'd be positioned by the window, looking out, waving. Every day she was on some new sort of medicine. My father and I kept up our side of the act - if my Uncle came to visit, my mother was just having a bath, she would be out in half an hour, shall we all go for a drive, and give her some time to herself? When

Aunty Susan drove down from Enderby, Mum had just popped out to get some milk to bake bread (well you know how she loved to cook) could I take Rose for a coffee somewhere? Mother had to be alone when she baked. You know how she is, quirky old thing. At school, there was nobody to deceive, and nobody who would have been interested in the truth.

I reached in under my bed and pulled out a map of the country I had purchased from Bob's Bargain Bin in the fifth form. A red dot went down on the Heights above Shackleton. I marked a black trail between Shackleton and Enderby. Enderby received some nice yellow marks - potential targets. I was a man on the up. Tomorrow I would get the hell out. Up to Enderby and a new beginning.

*I close my eyes and I am spinning down a hole, faster and faster, through the crust of the earth, covered up with lava and down to the molten core.*

All my dreams, then, are of fire.

*** 

Nobody in Enderby owns a garden; it is one out of control garden that owns the city. Or perhaps one creeper. This creeper grows over everything, smothering neat rows of roses, lovingly planted bulbs, potted geraniums and the occasional small dog. Only mad old women attempt to fight the creeper. No matter how it is chopped, or by whom, the creeper always comes back. This is the soul of the city - this chaotic force-to-be-reckoned with. It is the sum total of the all the greenery in the area - the backbenchers grouping together and overthrowing the government. There is no point in cultivating a small backyard plot. The creeper will come, perhaps from your neighbour's garden, or from the park at the back of the house, and wreak vengeance upon all that you have worked upon. Topiarists, horticulturalists, landscape gardeners across the city throw down their rakes in despair, empty hands held high to the heavens. I knew the creeper to be a sign. A great sign. The force of the city was already in place; all I had to do was tap into it, and I, too, would be spreading roots far and wide.

I spent that first night, a rainy Sunday in April, huddled in a bus shelter with an alcoholic and his gas stove. Financial situation: desperate. The week's dole had been blown on kerosene. I had also purchased a scrapbook and one hundred copies of the newspaper which had done the write-up on the fire up at the Knight's; neatly chopping out every article and making an extended collage which covered the first sixteen pages of the book; both sides. Never had I felt such pride.

When the alkie finally fell asleep, I took the newspaper which covered his lower body and scanned the situations vacant. How could a man like myself be of service? What more could I do for my country than I burn it to a cinder? The bum shuffled and groaned in his sleep.

"Jerome", he exhaled.

Oh dear God, if you spare me anything, spare me from having to listen to the tired old fantasies of a worn out loser.

"Jerome, rub it harder", he murmured, louder than before.

I coughed, twice, violently, to try and awaken him.

"Rub it Jerome."

I switched my ears onto off and kept my eyes vigilantly upon the column I was reading. IT Manager, computer programmer, computer sales, *Jerome*, Microsoft word 6.0, salary $40, 000, salary $50,000, *Jerome*, salary $60, 000, dos, *Jerome*, word for windows, *Jerome*. I rolled up the newspaper into a tight wad and swatted the offender about the face. He moaned enthusiastically and rolled over. Christ, it was freezing. On the street, the rain teamed down so hard, each drop shot back a fountain skywards. The streetlamps seemed to streak into the watery atmosphere; the sky was raining yellow light. My eyes travelled upwards on the page.

Cleaner, full-time, cleaner part-time, fish factory requires cleaner, childcare, trained in early childcare, nannying position available, live-in position. Who better qualified to look after children than an arsonist? I smiled softly to myself, knowing I had found my niche. And I know what you, dear reader, are thinking.

Why should she trust her children to a psychopath? For the simple reason, my sweet one, that yours truly was becoming increasingly skilled in the art of dressing up. Just as I could don the pyromaniac's costume, so also could I adopt the belligerent snigger of the nanny. The gregarious, fun-loving, small town man, just moved to the city, eager for employment. Able to dance, sing, paint and read stories to a (marginally) above average standard; years of childcare experience. Babysitting for Mrs ----- at age fourteen, child-minding for Mrs------ at age fifteen, tossing a rugger ball round with the next door neighbour's budding All Black sons, teaching -------- and ------ -- the best method for baking a mean nutty fruit scone.

References? But of course. Thirty or forty of the things. At least, I would have, as soon as the stationery shop opened and I could purchase ten different coloured pens. God would look after his own.

Pity I was not among their ranks.

## *Employment*

In the nursery, I sat at the old school table.  Looking down, the initials were carved so deep, it seemed there was more space than wood.  The curtains in the room were maroon plush-velvet, tied back with two black ribbons.  The walls were painted a lighter shade of maroon.  The room felt more like the banqueting hall of my anaesthetic nightmare visions than a child's playroom.  That's what money can do for your children.  They can be born adults; plum in the mouth when talking, silver spoon in the mouth when eating.  I felt myself the perfect man to raise such children.  Someone from the 'other side' as it were; the other side of the wealth division, the other side of the class division, the other side of the great divide which separates here from there.

On the phone, I had pulled it off superbly, a private school accent, well-rounded vowels.    Problems of homelessness and unemployment would be solved.  Just what I needed - a nice little day job to keep my hands and mind occupied until such time as they could be put to better use.   I crossed the room, and opened the window on a warm grey, drizzling sort of a day.  At this point, I figured, I could take a break from the burning.  Work for a couple of months, get some money together, and then inflict myself upon Enderby.

The Wilkeses were both executives; busy, over-worked, stress-loaded suckers for every new gimmick that hit the market.  In the kitchen; Easy-Yo, Nutri-Plan, Special K, Multivitamins For Him, Multivitamins For Her, Multivitamins For Under Fives, Multivitamins For Under Tens, Multivitamins for Teens, Black and Decker Bread Boy, Julia Childs' Ever Sharp Knife Set.  In the bathroom; Grecian 5000, Regain, Nutrigenics Anti-Aging Cream For Lids (toilet lids? jar lids? ), Cellulite Dissolving Gel, Blackmore's Blueberry Mask (dessert treat for the kids?).  In the bedroom; push-up bras, jockey extra support for him, Yuri Neglijev's Guide For Advanced Souls, Tina Turner's Recipe For Little Girl Legs, (Cajun spices and doll limbs?), magazines with their feature articles (*How To Win That Promotion, How To Dress*

*To Please Your Man, How To Tell If He's Sleeping Around, How To
Sleep Around, How Tone A Tummy, How To Bake Blancmange*).

The children seemed luxuriously unaware of the consumer
neuroses which pervaded the house, naively unafraid of the Easy-
Yo and the Black and Decker Bread Boy. Myself, I had the opposite
reaction. Just a glimpse of an electric egg slicer was enough to make
me break out in a cold sweat. This had long been the case. I lived
in fear of the age I was caught in. It was as if I had slept too long in
the sun, and awoken to find that history had sped ahead without
me. Catastrophe had happened while I dozed; the consumer war was
fought with weapons I could neither comprehend nor operate. It was
Shackleton that had been caught sleeping; Enderby had sped away
on its own - an out of control electric train with no conductor.

In spite of my fear of historical advancement, my job was
relatively easy. None of the twenty-four hour thought patterns
required for pyromania. The children, a three year old girl and a
seven year old boy, won me over. As their parents struggled for
conductorship of the technological train, the children had been
foisted from relative to relative, from family friend to family friend,
until, eventually, growing tired and feeling exploited, relatives and
friends had suggested a nanny. Prompted by the spate of killer
female nanny movies hitting the theatres, the Wilkeses had their
hearts set on a male. A sensible choice, I had to agree. I had been
the second interviewee, the first having been a junkie who'd had to
take a break during the vigilant interview to go and shoot up. With
my impeccable accent, bright shiny eyes and fifteen well written
references, they had hired me on the spot. Suckers. Of course, I
would not harm their children. I would act the perfect
nanny. Friendly yet professional; playful, yet disciplinary when
discipline was called for.

I had little or nothing to do with the 'man of the house'. He was
out of the place by seven every morning, would come home and
retire to his study. I was not to be treated as a butler; I was never
summoned, or sent for, or asked to be of service. I would hear him
through the walls; a shuffling of feet from the upstairs rooms, a
muffled cough, the tapping of a pen against paper.

It was Mrs Wilkes who ran the household, and as I came under
the category 'home', she also ran me. She was the kind of mother I

had constructed fantasies around, when my own mother was yelling at the television set, or chain-smoking as she prepared the evening's black pudding, or spitting out the upstairs window at those who came to the door to spread the good word. Mrs Wilkes was the kind of mother a young boy could show off to his friends; the kind of woman that other teenagers would develop a secret crush upon. Her hair was streaked, immaculate, and bobbed about her shoulders in a way which instantly endeared me to her. Her figure was voluptuous and her eyes the blue of the deepest ocean.

She was impossibly equine. Her personality contained within it all the qualities I admired in a good horse. A strong yet gentle personality, stamina - (the ability to last the distance, leap over high jumps and miscellaneous hurdles), good grooming and a kind of girlish spirit summed up in the tossing of a mane.

Shona, my mother and the eggs, my incompetent father, my pitiful arsonry; all were half a world away now. I had stepped into the realm of my dreams; that life of upper-class suburbia inhabited by Mrs Wilkes and all her over-dressed friends.

And my charges? Red-headed Lydia, the three year old, was blessed with her mother's horsy features, and a personality which charmed the proverbial pants. The seven year old, Keith, was not so much Lydia's sibling, as her nemesis. Every angelic action of Lydia's was mirrored by one of Keith's torturous acts. If Lydia saw fit to wrap her tiny arms around me and give me a hug, Keith took it upon himself to give me a vengeful boot in the shins. It was the small things in life which delighted him. The yanking of wings off butterflies, the stealing of the nanny's underwear, the chopping of his sister's hair. The lady of the house seemed oblivious to her son's behavioural problems. To her he was the darling baby boy, the bonny son. And, certainly, he could turn on the charm when it was called for.

His act was more transparent then a newly cleaned glass window. He would be out in the garden, beating up Lydia with a dry old stick, and the minute I would begin to reproach him, he would throw the stick upon the ground and holler blue murder. It was I, then, who was seen in the eyes of the family, to have been the torturer. It was only Lydia who was consistently on my side. Of course, she was too young to defend me to her parents, but she sensed my innocence and knew for certain of her brother's tyranny. Seven-year old Keith ruled the house through his cunning acts of manipulation. He left small surprises in unexplored rooms: a skinned frog in the spare bathroom, a cardboard sheet of pinned and mounted moths in the junk room upstairs, a pickled lamb's foetus on a dusty shelf in the attic. Just as each repulsive act of Keith's surpassed all his previous accomplishments, so Lydia continued to shine, pure and absolute. Blundering through the house in search of Keith, I would come across Lydia, perched upon the edge of a chair, singing to an empty room. She would turn around suddenly, and giggle, as if I had caught her doing something immoral or illegal; though she was too young to understand either concept. She didn't seem at all traumatized by Keith's acts of violence, and was calm to the point of docility when he chopped her hair/decapitated her dolls/spat into her food. I suspected that she was autistic, for how else could she swallow what she did without regurgitation?

Besides her inability to respond to trauma, she had just one trait that frightened me. She rocked. She rocked as she sang, she rocked as she ate her dinner, she rocked as I read to her from a Golden Book. This was not the possessed, zombie-like rocking of an idiot, but rather, the slow and thoughtful rocking of some Grandpa sitting out on the front porch in his favourite chair, cigar in mouth, the sun setting behind the house in a haze of yellow light. In short, this was the rocking of an old person, not some cutesy three year old. Her nature scared me as much as it charmed.

I reflected back upon my own acts of destruction. Christ I had been an idiot. The jobs had been messy, very messy. God only knew why I hadn't been caught, thrown in a cell, and tortured by some Nazi policemen with a thing for white boys. With nice little girls like Lydia around, you couldn't afford to fuck up. What if she was watching the news and saw some man being arrested for arson? She could be scarred for life. Far better that she see whole cities on fire, miscellaneous towns dissolving into flame, than see a man who had tried to light and failed.

# EPISODE FIVE

## *Mrs Wilkes*

As you well know, Enderby is South of Shackleton, and is more inclined to ice over in the winter. The Wilkeses were fine sporting types (as her looks suggested, Mrs Wilkes rode frequently). Curling, skiing, tobogganing, ice-skating - my job involved them all. I enjoyed my work. Oh please! Don't think I had forsaken my true vocation so easily, for I still dreamt of fire. Every night, my mind's eye would play me scene after scene of crumpling houses and burning rooms. During the daylight hours I banished such thoughts of destruction from my vision, and concentrated on taming Keith and tending to Lydia. For obvious reasons, I kept my distance from Keith. He was everything that I, as a seven year old, had not been. Gregarious, extroverted, destructive. Well, for sure, I may have developed into the King Of Fire, but as a young child I had been reserved, reticent, retiring. What would happen to the monster as he grew? His school reports suggested he was the classroom terrorist. Would he move on into the world, acting as he did, ruling by fear? He was the sort of person I was born to burn. And Lydia was the type I was born to save.

I still found it hard to believe that I had pulled everything off. I wore my nanny mask day and night, yet, sometimes, I would have nightmares. Mrs Wilkes would enter the room dressed in black, make her seductive way across the room to my bed, kick off her shoes and lie down beside me. We would embrace briefly, and then she would lean across and whisper softly in my ear, "I see through your disguise", which I would take for an amorous advance. Just as she began to bend her form over mine, I would feel two cold hands tearing at my face, the skin would be pulled away, and there Lady Wilkes would be, peering at all my nothingness. I would raise my own empty hands, as if to cover myself, but there my face would be; Cyclopean, unblinking.

*O the horror of being unmasked.*

37

One morning I had a vision. Well there I was, just lying on my back, staring at the ceiling and attempting to summon the courage to get out of bed and tackle a Saturday with Keith, when who should come shivering out of the plaster but my old Mum. She had equipped herself for an afternoon watching the soaps; gin bottle in one hand, rollers in the hair, fluffy bunny slippers - all the clichés. She hovered a while, quite close to the ceiling and then descended upon me as a swooping vulture would. A nasty shrieking filled my ears. I hadn't known she was dead, so the whole thing gave me a bit of a turn. Noticeably, my hands began to quake. She moved her lips and began to speak in Latin.

This was a stupid move on her part. She knew I didn't speak Latin. This was just like her, trying to prove her one-upsmanship. I got quite angry, then, and I think I may have begun to yell at her to stay away. Couldn't she just go home now that she was dead? Why did she have to keep hanging around like a filthy odour? She was practically right on top of me by this time; a wet dank smell came where she hovered, and she was as cold as ice. I knew that she had a message for me (why else do ghosts pay visits?), but her playing at guest was totally pointless if she insisted in screeching in that incomprehensible Latin. I batted ineffectually at the air. Still she hung. Sotto voce, I begged her to speak in English.

"All right then ya stupid little shit!", she screeched. "I haven't come back from the grave for nothing, you know!"

I curled my body into the foetal position, hoping that this might placate her.

"Straighten up when I'm talking to you!"

"Sorry Ma."

"I know what you're planning! I know what acts of destruction you have in mind! You're a sick boy!"

"Sorry Ma."

"You're sick to stay here with these little kids when you could be out getting a name for yourself. I didn't raise no son of mind to sit around at home and change the diapers! I've come to tell you son, you'd better get out there in the real world and do dome bloody damage before it's too damn late."

"Yes Ma, sorry Ma."

"Bad things will happen if you stay with the Wilkeses."

"I don't like bad things Ma."

"So get out of this ditch boy!  Your father and I have been watching, and we know that you're wasting your life.  So get your shit together son, or I'll bring your old Dad down here as well, and oh brother will he have a piece of your hide!"

"Dad?"

"A car accident son.  Your father fell asleep at the wheel and we went over the edge of a cliff."

At least she had said she'd bring Dad down.  I mean, if she'd said, "get your shit together or I'll bring your father up" I would have been kind of worried.  At this stage in the game, my father appearing before me drenched in hell-fire would have been more than I could have coped with.

"It's only temporary", was what I said.

"*Temporary* is what they all say.  And then before you know it, temporary has become permanent, and all you've got is your nine-to-five and too tired to do the real work.  Face facts.  You've always been bone idle.  Time you pulled finger."

"I need some money.  As soon as I've got some cash together, I'll be out through that doorframe like a flaming arrow."

"Bad        things        will        happen        if        you        stay."

"You've already warned me about the 'bad things'.  You're starting to sound like a stuck record."

She sniffed, and huffed her shoulders slightly.

"I suppose that's all the thanks a mother gets, is it?  I should have known.  Fine state things have come to when a mother can't even give her son some decent advice."

"I'm gonna do it Ma.  I'm gonna do the fire thing for you.  You just have to give me a bit of time."

"Your father and I have been waiting far too long for you to immortalise this family.  You'd better get your shit together."

"Come on Ma.  The world is my oyster."

"You got your oyster to open yet Boyo.  You might find a pearl, and you might find a piece of shit."

And on that parting note, she began to glow.  Her skin bleached itself, she became whiter and whiter before my eyes, and began to ascend in a blaze. I averted my stare. She passed through the ceiling as if it were no more solid than a sheet of paper.

I lay on my back for another minute, staring at the space through which she had exited, and then I decided to phone home, just to make sure she hadn't been tricking me about Dad. After all, she wasn't so long out of the hospital.

In the hallway I stood, receiver to ear, listening to the continued ring, on and on and on and never any reply. And then I pushed the hang-up button with my finger, and kept my ear tuned in to the noise of nothing. I let go of the button and heard the dial tone resume its position as guardian of the phone line; a stream of white blank sound.

\*\*\*

My mother's prophesy of doom tainted my life. Whom would catastrophe deign to point its crooked finger towards? Would Lydia's rocking prove to be her eventual undoing? Would the lady of the house take one Nutri-Plan too many? I lived a life of constant fear. I began to re-map my career. At night, I would spend hours pouring over a map of Enderby, again re-charting my intended movements. I changed my colour code. Black for unburnt areas, orange for potential targets and red for successful hits. I refocused. My mother was right. I had become somewhat distracted from my calling. I resolved to dedicate all spare time to the cause.

The death of my parents did not much perturb me. To tell the truth, I was kind of glad to have them out of the picture. Although they were not so much out of the picture as sitting on the ledge of the frame, legs dangling over the edge, looking on, frowning. Still they would be forced to wait. A man could only do so much with his time. There was no point in him running himself into the ground.

\*\*\*

Of course, they were not forced to wait. Apocalypse struck. Mothers are always right. I had packed the children up for a pleasant day upon the ice, blades swung over shoulders, spare hands clutching brown paper bags containing lunches.

At noon, the sun came out, and the thaw began.   Lydia and I spread a chequered blanket, and sat on the bank which rose above the pond, eating egg rolls and watching Keith as he skated farther out upon the lake. Our skins were itching, burning and beginning to peel. Keith skated on across the ice. Lydia picked at the skin on the end of her nose.  I took another bite of my egg roll and by then he had gone too far out, I had told him not to go so far.

I was yelling at him from the bank, and then he was standing, stretched face glaring back at me, the cracks splitting out beneath his feet. Lydia and I stood on the bank, watching in terror, the blood pumping splinters of ice through our veins. And then he was under, his face pushed up against the underbelly of the ice, eyes glassy with fear, fish-gill mouth opening and closing.  Skin an embryonic pink. Arms outspread, beating the lucid ice; the wings of an angel. I called out his name, once, and my voice echoed out around the valley,   then   ricocheted   back   upon   itself;   an   impotent boomerang.  His movements slowed as he grew colder.  His mouth moved to a more leisurely beat.

On the bank, Lydia rocked. We ran.

## *Missing*

I took her with me. Withdrawing my savings in Enderby, we bought a sky-blue Mark II Zephyr with crème vinyl seats. "Where's Mummy", she'd cry, "where's Mummy", and I would buy her ice-creams, stuffed bunny rabbits, lollies, chocolate chip biscuits, Barbie dolls, toy guns. I was determined to take the life of the Knights and the Wilkeses with me. I was determined to steal what I was not given. How could I leave my ingénue behind me? I felt fear chasing me, genuine fear, hot panting breath down the back of my shirt collars, etc. We sped down the main road out. My mother took it upon herself to have her tuppence worth.

"What the hell! Did I tell you to steal the kid? Did I raise my son to be a child stealer? I don't think so. And what have you done? You've gone and stolen this beautiful girl from her happy home."

"There's a lump rising in my throat Ma, really."

"Cut the lip boy. Is this theft going to help you to get some good flame going? No. No no NO! I drowned that boy especially for you, and now you've gone and stuffed it all up. That boy was nothing but..."

"Come on, Mother, he didn't deserve to die!"

"He was a shit! A right little shit. Anyway, I didn't see you rushing out onto the ice to save him."

"Give us a break!"

"I have! And you've gone and stuffed it up. They'll be after you now, hounds yapping at your heels. There'll be no escape. They'll want to make you pay. They'll want to see you dead. This kidnapping stint's gonna make your life one hundred per cent harder Boyo."

She knew that I detested being called Boyo.

"I just want you too know that I'll be watching you, son. No matter where you travel and no matter who you travel there with, you can guarantee that your father and I will be watching. Remember - you stuff up and it reflects real badly on the family name. We've got that bloke you burnt on our side as well, and Keith sends his fondest regards. Lord knows how he made his way inside here. Suffer the little children and all that, I guess. Anybody who dies by your hand wants you to achieve immortality - they figure that way they might be remembered along with you."

It occurred to me that perhaps lunacy did not vacate the dearly departed at the morgue. Had Ma checked in past St Peter, psychoses tucked away in handbag? Had she conned the lift operator into pressing his thumb against the up arrow, rather than the deserved down? So her presence contained three other deaths; my father, the burning man and the frozen boy. She spoke on behalf of the dead.
"Burn on our behalf, boy. Burn for the dead ones, the ones that will never be remembered; those that froze and the ones that drowned and those that died silent and unacknowledged deaths. Let us take you to hell and back."
"Who said I wanted to travel?"
I turned my neck to face her and felt the breeze of airy nothing.

Lydia was swinging her legs and sucking contentedly at a packet of sherbet. All my plans, my carefully constructed maps, tore themselves to shreds before my blinking inner eye. We could not have remained in Enderby. Sure, my name would have been on a lot of walls - wanted posters, thirty million pictures of your humble narrator's ugly mug spread across the city. And a few thousand pictures of the little lady up, besides. We could never have rented in a city under those circumstances. God! I was destined to be homeless. For Shackleton was no longer any kind of hated haven now that my parents had absented themselves.

I had no home and it made me nervous. In fact, being alive made me nervous. I was a very nervy kind of a guy. The windowpane of the car would rattle and I would scream. Lydia would snap the stick of the lolly she was slurping on, and I would leap a mile into the air, leaving my skin sitting on the driver's seat beneath me. I thought of my life as if it were a movie. I was outside myself looking in - I did not like the dimly lit room that I saw. There were piles of dust in all four corners of the room, the door was locked, the paper hung dripping from the walls. The room was devoid of furniture.

Guilt made me hollow. I carried my crimes with me. No matter that I was not strictly responsible for Keith's drowning - it was I who had taken him ice skating, and stood, and watched him drown. It was not Keith who deserved to die; it was me. I thought of Mrs

Wilkes at home, weeping over her two absent children, and of Mr Wilkes, locking himself in his study and working incessantly, and I felt sick and empty and hated myself and wanted to die. I worked myself into this, lower and lower, and when I struck the rock at the bottom of the well, I felt something kicking and I knew that it was this kicking thing that made me what I was. An arsonist. No choice about it. From the empty well I drew new strength and conviction. My life had been a soft, fetid, melting, cheesy mess. I hadn't stuck by anything, not even my arson. Ma was right. At the first chance to escape poverty, I had run like a simpering weakling. Run to safety and comfort and a cute little job and a nice warm bed. Now things were rougher. I was, no doubt, a wanted man. About time. Time we saw some action.

"I want Mummy."

"We're just going on a little holiday, Liddy."

"My name's not Liddy. My name's Lydia."

Nothing is quite so embarrassing as a child refuting affectation.

"Where's Mummy?"

"We've left Mummy behind us, Sweetie."

"I want Keith."

Christ! And all the times he'd given her Chinese torture, smeared her sheets with blood from that night's prospective lamb roast and smacked her about the ears.

"Keith's passed on."

"But I want Keith."

No logic like want.

"You won't see Keith again."

"Why?"

"He's gone."

"But where's he gone."

"Up where the angels fly."

"What's angels?"

"Floaty things."

"What's floaty things?"

"Keith."

Fight kiddie questions with kiddie replies.

"Where are we going?"

"Away."

"Why?"

"Because I said. Would you like some more sherbet?"

Anything to shut her up.

   Ma descended through the roof.

"Not only have you stolen Lydia, but now you're going to insist on rotting her teeth for her as well."

"Face facts Ma. You know shit about shit. Sugar's good for kids. Keeps them smiling and satisfied, strong and healthy. Anyway, I hardly think you're in a position to criticize. Look what you raised. The King Loser, that's what you managed to bring up. Although 'managed' is perhaps entirely the wrong word to use here. Perhaps, 'struggled' or 'wrestled' would be more appropriate. And you fucked up, Momma, you fucked up big time."

"Don't you dare speak to your Mother like that. And don't you dream of using swear words ever again in your piddling little life."

She pulled the plug on my self-confidence, and I dribbled out down the drainpipe like so much rotting dishwater.

"And as for you being a 'fuck-up' (as you so eloquently put it), well I can only but agree with you. That's why I'm urging you to redeem yourself whilst there's still time. Make something of you life, my boy, and quickly, or I'll make a little pact with fate and it'll be game over. Let's not forget the icy end wee Keith came to."

I could not believe that own mother was threatening me with my death.

"And if you will insist on ripping that poor little girl from her Mother, you can at least treat her digestive tract with a little respect."

"Ha! I seem to recall a childhood happily filled with biscuits and jam tarts when a certain matriarch found herself otherwise occupied in watching soap re-runs or yet another American talkback show with a host who 'used to be fat' and then saw the light and now interviews...."

"Shut up and listen. I have a message from your father."

"Father?"

"From your Dad. He says that he's real proud of you for torching the Knight's place, because Mr Knight owed him seven thousand dollars. Unpaid electrician's expenses. And, also, Dad says the word on the street is that Mr Knight was rather too fond of his tax

dodges. And Mr Knight didn't have House and Contents Insurance, so he's pretty rooted. You did well. Keep up the good work, says Dad. But I say, son, get your arse into gear. You've only got a short while stalking this earth; best get the work done before you reach fifty. That way you can retire in peace, perhaps cultivate a small fertile garden or take up a hobby such as learning Spanish or cooking difficult Chinese dishes. Those won things..."
"Won-tons."
"Whatever. Settle down, get to know the area you live in. For Christ's sakes, you didn't spend more than a month in Enderby! You didn't even get to see the outer suburbs that you were so eager to burn. And now you're on the road to God Knows Where, no direction whatsoever. That's the thing you've always lacked, direction."
I sat in a small corner of my head and hummed, untouchable. Her words washed over me in waves, crashed in upon their own pebbly shores and rushed back out into the ocean. Radio static.
"So where do you intend to stay the night?"
I ignored her.
"I'm talking to you!"
My mouth remained glued shut.
"Hey! Cat got your tongue?"
"You're cracked Ma! No, not cracked, smashed, like a stack of porcelain plates dumped on the floor by a grumpy kitchen-hand. I can't believe you intend to control my life from beyond the grave. Do you realise how fucked that is?"
She grew sulky.
"I'm only trying to protect you."
"From what?"
"Yourself."
"You're the only thing I need protection from."
"You're your father's only son! I need to shelter you from the world that you're about to torch. I mean to say, boy, take a good long look at yourself. Left alone with your weaponry, you're all set to follow that age-old path of self-destruction mapped out by your ancestors."
"What ancestors?"
"Oh don't play coy with me. You know your genealogy. Our family stretches back to time memorial. Our little group has always been

and always will until the end. You've seen the family tree that hangs on the living room wall. So it's not just me that's counting on you son. It's the whole damned family. You'd better not let all us dead folks down."

I decided to humour her in her delusion.

"Sure Ma. Why don't you just go on back to that big old ocean in the sky and tell all the rellies there's no worries. Your little boy's got this earth thing sussed, no bones about it."

"We're depending on you, boyo."

I cringed. Boyo. She sure knew how to hit where it hurt.

"I appreciate the full extent of the responsibility Ma."

"So don't fuck up. I didn't spend large chunks of my life sitting on the sofa drinking gins and watching daytime television just so you could be a drop-kick."

I turned again, to look, and she was gone. That's my Ma. Forever hovering on the periphery of vision. Turn to stare straight at her, and you'll be staring at nothing. That's who she was - nothing. That's who she spoke for - all the dead nothings. The nothings that thought they were going to last. Suckers. I was the only nothing destined for immortality. Nameless fame, of course, now that I was nobody. I now realised - if they wanted to paste pictures of me across the city, they would be pasting blank paper; if they wanted to print my name, they would have to call me nameless. It wasn't my own name I wanted to write in flame, it was the names of my victims. Anyway, our family had no name. We were the Shackleton Family Nothing. They were putting a ridiculous amount of pressure on me. Just because they had slacked around in their own lifetimes, they expected me to make up for all that now. Still, for the sake of my own fate, it was best to play along with the game. With the dead on my side, who knew what might be accomplished.

Lydia was still doing the one track record impersonation.

"I want Mummy."

"No time to mourn the past Liddy."

"I'M NOT LIDDY."

Oh please, sweet one, no tantrum throwing. Time for some added placation.

"Chocolate chip?"

She puked up then, suddenly, without warning; a reservoir overflowing. Tears spilled down her cheeks. Shit. She was never like this at home.

"Oh come on Lydia, play the game."

"I don't want to play any games."

Was there a children's refuge centre anywhere? Could I leave her on the side of the road, bundled up in my old sweater, hoping that some kindly farming couple would stumble across her and take her home and feed her chicken noodle soup? Could I discreetly push her into a clothing bin and leave her there? I should have left her back there, on the side of the lake. She wasn't made for the road, that's for sure. Too soft for the hard criminal lifestyle I would soon be leading. Sending her home through the mailing system was too risky. Perhaps I could slip some courier twenty bucks and hope for the best? No way. Forget it. Too many perverts and psychos out there to trust this little girl to just anyone.

I shoved her a tissue to clean up the spew.

"I wanna go home", she wailed.

What had I been thinking of? This kid was going to ruin everything.

We pulled into a Motel Pteron. These classy joints were stationed all up and down the country. All the sofas were vinyl, all the TVs were stuck on static stations, all the jugs had busted elements. I like these motels. That's what this deal would be - a motel crawl.

The guy on reception was asleep when we arrived. Lydia had stopped crying. The puke was beginning to solidify. I held her upon my hip with one hand and gave Mr Reception-Sleepy a solid bash with the other. He rose up to meet my gaze, clutching onto his nose and looking far meaner than I had anticipated. Wakey wakey, rise and shine.

"Yo Mothafucka, you got a problem? You bash every man you meet?"

"Just a friendly wake-up tap."

"Tap! A tap? You call that a mother tap. That was a bash man, and you better realise that that's what that was. 'Cause you don't realise it in the next mother thirty seconds and I'm gonna tap your face."

Somebody had been watching too many Tarantino movies.

"All we want is a room for one."

"Then you ask, Mothafucka, and you ask nicely. You don't go on and bash somebody just 'cause he's got his eyes staring down at the desk, you hear what I'm saying."
"Loud and clear."
Through a side window which looked into an adjoining room, I was sure I caught a glimpse of a Pulp Fiction poster stuck up on the wall.
"I hope you're listening, man, 'cause I'm talking to you."
"No potatoes in my ears."
"What?"
"I'm listening."
"You and her want a room?"
I nodded. He tossed me a key. Another white boy from the ghetto.

Our room was in the basement. The walls were decorated with pieces of old clocks. Cogs, wheels, hands. Many of these had fallen off and lay broken upon the floor. The one window gazed out onto a concrete wall, and was so covered by cobwebs that looking wasn't worth the effort. Lydia picked up a cog and began chewing.
"Lydia!" I admonished, "dirty".
Great acting on my part. Relax, take a deep breath and just be Dad.
"I'm going to need your help Lydia."
Nonchalantly, she chewed.
"We're about to take on a big job."
I knelt on dusty floor and looked her dead in the eye.
"Lydia - I want you to be my fait accompli."
"I want Mummy", and the tears spilled down.
For the first time I realised how she was feeling. God, but I had been a selfish bastard. Ripping this poor little dear away from Mummy, driving her hundreds of miles from home, plying her with cookies and sweets......grown men have been jailed for less. I, too, began to weep. Yes, I, down there on the floor with that two year old, shed a bitter tear for out mutual fate. I had thought that we were blessed, but surely we were cursed. Again, she began to rock. This consoled the both of us. The uterine action calmed poor Liddy, while I, her guardian, took solace from the face that she was a self-comforting unit. Providing care for another was exhausting. I barely had the psychic strength to look after Number One.

She rocked and she rocked and, as will often be with children, tears led to sleep. She crashed out right there, upon the floor. I staggered over to the single bed and stretched myself upon its candlewick opulence. Somewhere, a dog barked. Sleep engulfed me.

# EPISODE SIX

## *Taxidermy*

Titan was my father's hometown. Born, bred and raised a Titanian, he would boast, and I would bow humbly to the Queen of the Fairies. He liked that bowing, but when he found out what I was calling him to Ma behind his back, he was pretty annoyed. We had left Titan for Shackleton when I was eleven. The memories I have of the city are all happy ones, 'cause that was all before my life took its downwards slide. The move to Shackleton had been the beginning of the end as far as family relations went. Long before my eighteenth birthday and the whole thing smashed, the porcelain plate that was my mother's sanity began to show large cracks and fissures. My father and I fared a little better. Dad had never had anything so fragile as a plate to smash in the first place, and my own supper dish survived the shift for the large part intact, with only one or two delicate hairline fractures.

This is what I can remember after the ice, when my past comes into focus.

We'd had a really nice big house in Titan, with awesome engravings in the plaster ceilings; juicy round grapes and fig leaves and naked angels and that sort of shit. We'd had a great dog back then too, Obadiah; a beautiful black lab. The best part about Obe was the fat rolls up by his neck. They were all soft and squishy and luxurious like a bit of plush velvet and you could grab his skin in a big roll and squeeze it and he wouldn't complain. If he was lying on the floor you could get down next to him with your head on his neck and he was the softest pillow you'd ever used. He didn't moan then either, 'cause he was totally docile. He was a really nice canine and the only dog I've ever really trusted.

There were lots of good kids up at Titan as well, not like the blockheads at Shackleton. My family weren't looked on as freaks up there, 'cause there was a big ethnic population and heaps of arty farty types.    We were pretty boring compared to most Titanians.  Titan was a miniature Vegas, and was the first city in the country to have a casino.  This was great.  Ma smuggled me inside there once and I had a couple of sips of her gin and tonic (which she then drank only in moderation) and she gave me a go at roulette.  We got some funny looks when we went gambling, 'cause I only just made four foot, but there were a few other dwarfs playing the games and serving drinks, so we weren't embarrassingly out of place.  The casino was a great big glitzy place with tons of neon and strobe and flashing lights and men in tuxedos and women in really short gold and silver skirts.  It was heavenly.  All the women seemed to have empty pockets, and all the men seemed to have bottomless pockets.  So the men played the games and the women played the men.  Whenever somebody's ship came in, dwarfs dressed up in cherub outfits would swoop down from the ceiling in gold harnesses strung onto invisible wires and blow on a couple of hot-pink plastic trumpets.  A cheer would go up from all the employees, and about thirty women would rush to see which eligible male had just won a large sum of dough.

A woman playing for herself was rare.  It wasn't that there weren't women in Titan with money, it was just that the dollars had usually been so hard won, that they wouldn't gamble with their money any more than they would with their own soul.  Occasionally you would see a rich women, dressed in black, gambling with her dead husband's loot; and then it would be she who was surrounded by admiring men, all eager to get a hand into her widow's purse.

When I look back now, just a flick of my head, the first ten years of my life seem utopian.  Then I turn and stare and look back harder and I imagine that I can sense the origins of some unnameable, inexplicable terror.  I think I can trace this fear to the demise of Obadiah, but I can never be sure.  Titan was nothing but great, I'm not denying that.  All I'm saying is if it hadn't been for the incident with Obe we might never have moved to Shackleton and everything would have been different.  Like they say, the past is another country.  But I don't necessarily have a passport to travel there.

I had some terrific mates in Titan, what my Ma would refer to as my "nice little friends".  I don't know that they were very 'nice', but we had some good times doing miniature burglaries on any old biddy who was stupid enough to think that we were kids of the "come in and have an Earnest Adams lamington" variety. Sadly, we were not these children. It just goes to show that I have always been attracted to liars, thieves, psychopaths, offenders and losers; that I have always craved the excitement of crime and criminals. This was part of the problem with moving to Shackleton; I had to straighten out and be a nice little boy and it didn't agree with me. It was me and three other little fellas that did it. We never did stuff physically, we just took advantage of elderly ignorance. It started when Mr Phripps-next-door invited me and one of the other boys over for a piece of orange cake that his niece had baked for him especially so he could entertain. He was real nice, Mr Phripps, and always let me pick leaves and stuff out of his garden when I was in the mood for nature.

Anyway, me and this other boy, Nathan, went into Mr Phipps' place and it really stank of cat's piss, but I guess he couldn't smell it 'cause he was so old and everything. I felt really sorry for him, and sat there with my mate while a canary in a wicker cage chirped like it wanted out and Mr Phripps spouted on and on and on about all his relations, most of whom, I suspected, were now dead, although he spoke about them as if they were still living. We sat on cushioned chairs. The orange cake was old and dry and stale and stuck in my throat when I tried to swallow. I picked all the icing off the top, but then I had to try and produce extra-ordinary amounts of saliva just so that I might get the stuff down my throat. When I was about halfway through my bit of cake, Nathan, (who had, through some supernatural act of salivation, finished all his), stood up and said he had to go to the bathroom to piss. Phripps didn't even blink twice at the use of the word; I doubt that he'd even heard what had been said, though he seemed to have picked up on the general gist of my mate's desire, 'cause he pointed down the hallway with a gnarled finger and moved the conversation on to tell me all about his old Mum who was going a bit batty. This was the year before we shifted, so I was only about ten, and Phripps scared the shit. He had a mouth like a high-speed motor, and he talked incessantly, until I was down to my last bit of cake. Nathan still hadn't returned, and I was getting dead worried. I couldn't quite finish my cake either; my mouth felt as though it had been blasted out with a paint-scraper. I moved slightly on my chair, shoved the piece of cake under the cushion and then repositioned myself. Phripps had changed to topic to his Dad, who also had bats in the belfry. Just as I was considering panicking, Nathan appeared in the room with a large bulge protruding out the front of his jacket. He motioned with his head towards the door. I thanked Mr Phripps for the lovely cake and followed my mate outside. I couldn't believe it. He'd nicked this revolting alabaster statue from Phipps' corridor. A thrill ran through me. This kind of thing would make great presents for parental birthdays.

So that was how the whole racket started. We nice little boys'd pair off and play befriend an ancient, get invited around for something sweet and stale, then do a bit of small-time fleecing. I always went with Nathan, since he'd been the one to start the whole thing off and he seemed to know what he was doing. We never took anything they'd notice; just small tricks we could give away to our own relatives or use to decorate the dining room. We only did it about once a week. It was a Friday evening routine for me; nick off with something worthless. I'd usually go back to the house and feel a bit stink about it. So I'd stick a leash around Obe an take him for a big long walk so as I'd return home feeling all cleansed for a good night in front of the telly.

We only ever made one mistake, but it was that mistake, made during the long and boring summer holidays that fucked up everything. It was this old rich bastard I'd seen at the casino that time I'd been with Ma; women practically hanging off each wrinkle. He was shouting them all drinks, and giving out tokens like they were lollies. I'd thought he'd have so much expensive stuff in his house that he was worth taking a risk on. Up till then we'd only targeted those safely within the senility bracket, but Margeson was so well off we'd thought he was worth breaking a rule for. He lived about two blocks from our house, in an old crumbling mansion with an expansive, rolling green lawn.

Nobody knew much about Margeson; how he'd come by his money, or how he spent his time. Nathan and I decided that, being a bit of a challenge, the old bastard would be best left to us. Upon hearing that they'd be left out of the action, I think our mates were more relieved than disappointed. Me and Nathan began taking surreptitious walks past the rich man's house, trying to look famished in order that he would take pity on us and invite us inside for a bit of lamington. I'd take Obadiah with me, so he'd get a bit of exercise, and we'd stroll up and down, looking expectantly for the absent man, but there was never any sign. After a week of near constant walking, Nathan plucked up the courage to knock on Margeson's front door, pretending to be collecting for the Crippled Children's Society.

We shoved some leaves into a brown paper bag so that it looked as if we'd had some donations from others in the neighbourhood and Nathan walked right up to the front door and bashed with the lion's head knocker. The sky was black. Obe and I were hiding in some bushes about ten metres from the front door, so when Margeson himself came out and talked to Nathan, I could see right down the corridor. To one side of the doorway was a glass conservatory, which had been tacked onto the rest of the house, and was cloaked by heavy drapes. I could hear Nathan spouting on about tetraplegia, and behind Margeson I could see what looked like the fur-lined walls of the hallway. A cat was meowing around Matheson's ankles and he reached down to give the thing a pat. Behind him, I caught a glimpse of white fang.

*It doesn't have to be the end for these young children*, Nathan was saying. *Together we can envisage a brighter future.*

Verbose bastard, always winning the English prizes. Margeson's mouth was moving, but I could not hear what he was saying. It must have been an invitation to enter, for Nathan went inside and Margeson closed the door behind them. I stayed crouched where I was, fully prepared to race to the police if the plan stuffed up. The curtains were being drawn in the conservatory and I could see the inside of the extra glass room. Nathan was standing where the added glass joined the rest of the house. I couldn't see the expression on his face. The room was filled with stuffed animals of all shapes and descriptions. Ferrets carrying baby birds in their mouths were frozen mid-stride; penguins stood astride cardboard ice-floats; an otter lay before a lake of mirror and tinfoil, forever preparing to take a timeless plunge. Beside me, Obadiah whimpered. I saw Nathan backing from the room, while Margeson picked up the otter and sat it on top of the lake. He continued playing with his toys until Nathan appeared at the door, looking a little pale. He was clutching something under his jacket; Margeson was looking at us through the glass of the conservatory.

*What a score!* said Nathan, as we were backing away. *A brass housefly.*

He pulled the catch out from where he had been holding it. I feigned approval.

*You're right Nath. It's ace!*

*Look at the way it's preening itself,* said Nathan. *That's one in a million, that is.*

Fuck it was ugly. It had one front leg up by its fly-snout, 'preening', as Nathan had suggested.

*Your Ma'll love it*, I said, feverishly praying that I wouldn't be expected to take it home.

He had the best collection of this sort of shit I've ever seen in my life.

*I saw it*, I said.

Obe was trying to jump up to get at the fly.

*Down boy.*

He snarled. I looked back over my shoulder and saw that Margeson was standing in the doorway, yelling soundlessly. The black sky broke and we started to run.

That night I had some terrible nightmares. I dreamt that my feet were stuck in mud, and that I could not run, though I was being chased by an invisible enemy. I dreamt that I was awake and walking down a hallway towards the telephone, but when I picked up the black receiver, there was nothing on the other end of the line. I dreamt that I was cast in lead.

## Prison Potential

I don't know why it is, but supermarkets have always inspired me to new heights of dread. Perhaps it is the abundance of consumer choice, perhaps it is the frantic rushings and pushings of the other customers, perhaps it is the bored and pimply checkout girls. I seem to always find myself lurking in the fish section, somewhere near the smoked salmon (which I have no hope in hell of affording) pointing wildly at some fresh mussels (which I hate). Supermarkets are a death-trap for punters like me. Fish, hook, line and sinker I am always done in. Mars Bars; three for a dollar (I hate Mars Bars but they are nice and healthy for Liddy), Plain Pack Tampons a bargain at $4.95 a box of sixteen (What would I do with tampons? Aid a damsel in distress?), rice wafers, $1.99 for ten (there's plenty of polystyrene in the boot of the car).

On this morning, Lydia in tow, I whistled to reassure myself. As always, panic began to rise within my chest. I began to sing for added comfort. Quite loudly, actually. People stared. I freeze, mid-note. Damn. How humiliating. Furtively, I searched the back files of my brain for the food substance I required. Morning, breakfast, muesli. And stewed apple for the girl. Retiring to a safe whistle, I found the goodies and headed for the checkout with the shortest queue.

"Lydia?"

*Jesus where is she?*

"Lydia sweetie?"

People shot me looks of pity, contempt, helplessness. I peered down the first aisle; looming stacks of canned fruit and vegetables, packet mix soups, dried pasta. My movements grew more frantic. I searched aisle after aisle; Knights Castle soap, Brillo scrubbing pads, Hygenix dishcloths, Fancy Wrap Panty Liners. Oh God. I got down on my knees, there on the supermarket floor and began to pray. *Father who art in heaven, hallowed be thy name and something something something thy will be done on earth as something something.* Words escaped my lips.

"Lilly come back to your Poppa."

A small blonde woman in blue jeans and a crème sweater grabs my elbow.

"I'm sorry. Are you alright?"

"My girl.....my little baby."

"Have you lost somebody?"

I pull myself together.

"Yes. A small female child, three years old, about two foot high....."

"What colour is her hair?"

Colour, hair colour, colour of hair. Shit. My eyes scanned the dye packets.

Ash blonde? Strawberry blonde? Superblonde? Brilliant.....

"Red", I said.

"Pale skin?"

"LADY! OF COURSE SHE'S GOT PALE SKIN! SHE'S A REDHEAD! OF COURSE SHE'S GOT PALE SKIN! IT'S SO PALE IT'S ALMOST TRANSPARENT!"

A man began to approach. Pinned to his chest was a badge that said, "Barry. Trainee Manager."

"Alright, alright. I was only trying to help. No need to rip my head off."

She lowered her voice a tone.

"Bloody psycho."

"What seems to be the problem here?"

"Rack off Barry."

"He's lost his daughter."

"I haven't lost her. I've just misplaced....."

"What's she look like?"

"He started yelling about red hair. But he might well be lying."

"LYING!?"

Barry asserted his manhood.

"Just calm down Sir. I'm sure we'll find your daughter."

"Why would I lie, eh? Just give me one good reason why I would want to lie about the colour of her goddamned hair!"

"Please, Sir. Moderate your language. This is a family supermarket."

"Now you listen to me, Barry, and you listen real closely. I have lost a little girl somewhere in this place, and it's your job, if you want to make it to Manager, to find her. I want you to check everywhere, Barry. Leave no can of tuna unturned."

Barry nodded sagely. The blonde woman was whispering in his ear. Barry took me by the elbow and lead me up the managerial stairs. I was pushed into a small yellow room decorated with nudy pics of women on bikes. A newspaper was examined. Police were called. Words were bandied about like shuttlecocks. Molesterer, murderer, pervert, lunatic. I kept a stiff upper lip. A newspaper was held up next to my face as they compared me to some ugly bastard that's wanted by the boys in blue.

"I think we've found our man. Many thanks."

Obviously Barry had done something a little bit naughty. I whistled a happy tune.

"Lydia's been sent home", said Barry.

And I was led away.

# EPISODE SEVEN

## *Coppers*

How had it all gone wrong so quickly? I knew the answer lay with my mother, so intent on revenge. Matriarchs can be so selfish.

The police treated me pretty nicely. Nobody kicked me in the guts as I lay crumpled on the floor, nobody beat me about the head with a baton, nobody pissed or shat upon my prone form. They handed me a cuppa and a chicken sandwich. The sandwich was revolting. More butter than bird. The lard hung together in large chunks of grease. I tried, but I couldn't swallow. I knocked back the cuppa and stuffed the sandwich into my inside jacket pocket. You never know when you're gonna get desperate. Waste not want not.

Copper One approached me.

"Watching too many Hollywood movies, eh? *Hand That Rocks The Cradle* and all that?"

I tittered, demurely.

"You a queer, boy?"

He twiddled a pen between his teeth.

"No."

"No what?"

"No mister."

"No sir. Do you hear me?"

"Yes mister."

"Don't you get impudent with me boy!"

If there's one thing I detest in this world, it's a little man with power. I don't mind the big guys so much, the ones that're running the whole show, the politicians and the Heads of Department and the blokes down at the Pentagon; it's the little fellas that get me. The barman who won't serve another drink, the bouncer on the door of some cheesy little cabaret-style nightclub, the library clerk charging you three dollars fifty just to put a book on reserve. All the little fuckwits who won't bend the rules for their own disgusting little anal reasons. This chap fit right in to the picture. He put his pen down on the desk, right next to my file. And then I saw him actually straighten his pen, so that it was parallel with the file. I knew I was in deep trouble. Any man that bothers to straighten his pen is bound to have it in for a chaotic guy like me. I reassured myself. What did they have on me, really? Nobody knew about the arson. All that had happened was that the kid had drowned, and I had done a runner. Nothing criminal, I just hadn't been thinking straight. Kidnapping? Far from it. It was just instinct officer, to run, though no crime had been committed. I had been intending to return Lydia home the next day, and give in my notice. The shame was too much, officer. Though I had not encouraged him out on the ice during the thaw, I still felt the guilt that a parent would. I'm like that officer, a real nice guy. I feel for everybody; can I help that? Sensitive, officer. That's me. Just flipped out when the kid was under and freezing, didn't know what to do, just ran with the girl. Molestation? What kind of monster do you think I am? She's only three years old for Pete's sakes and I don't do none of that cradle snatching stuff. No I don't watch those Hollywood films. No cradle rocking and no cradle robbing. Oh please officer not the overnight cell, well, I have not done any wrong thing. Just ring the Wilkeses, they'll testify on my behalf. They've been phoned? Always a bit suspicious, that's just rubbish, I've served them well. Oh come on, they loved me. You know that they loved me. At times it was as if I were their adopted son. Their own son officer, that's how close we were, me and Mrs Wilkes. Like peas in a pod. Like this (two fingers tightly crossed). Mr Wilkes? He was different. Kept to himself did Mr Wilkes. Barely a peep out of that one. Just the odd upstairs shuffle and the random hacking cough. Sure we didn't speak much, but I never did anything to arouse his suspicions. I was the perfect hired boy. Polite, yet not overfriendly, reserved, yet not aloof, oh hell manslaughter but I'm not guilty oh shit molestation but I never touched her oh god what am I supposed to do?

In keeping with the spirit of the family, I black out cold upon the hard concrete floor.

## Rose

I didn't like many of the people in Shackleton, but I had once had a friend. This was before the year before high school started, when I liked people better. I had not done anything to encourage Savy. He just started talking to me the day that he arrived at our school, and then followed me down to the bottom field at lunchtime. I guess he hadn't had enough time in Shackleton yet to work out that I was a loser who didn't want to make friends with nobody. I was pretty pissed that he'd started to talk to me, 'cause all I asked from the other people at my school was that they left me alone. The kids at Titan had been much better than these dropkicks; I'd had quite a few mates before I moved to Shackleton.

The main reason I eventually started responded to Savy's blithering was 'cause he was the new boy and I knew what that felt like. I'd been at my school for ten months now, and in that time I'd only spoken to about two or three people. If you didn't play rugby you were in for a pretty hard time. Nobody gave me any shit though, and I had a reputation for being a bit of a psychopath after I'd accidentally stabbed a lab rat with a pen-knife during a science lesson on my second day at school. Some of the blood had sprayed out onto the back of Loris Knight's skirt and she'd screamed and flapped her arms about like a chook with its head cut off.

Savy arrived at school on a good day, 'cause we had some lunchtime entertainment that the teachers didn't know about. The entertainment was Rosemary, the school performer who put on a free show down by the gum trees at the end of the bottom field. She only performed on Mondays and Fridays, so Savy was pretty fortunate to arrive on a day when she was doing her thing. For obvious reasons, Rosemary was hated by all the other girls, but popular among the boys. I had nothing but respect for her; she was the only girl at school who didn't continually suck up to Loris and the rest of that crowd. She was her own woman, and, as it later turned out, she had quite a head for business. There was a fairly large gathering of guys by the time that me and Savy got down there, so we'd had to climb up one of the gums to get a view. Rose's performance was a bit weak, she was only lifting her skirt up and turning around like a girl inside a music box; it was pretty disappointing. On other occasions she'd been known to do cartwheels so that her top would fly up as well as her skirt. She was quite well developed for a twelve year old. She'd had on my favourite knickers though; a nylon navy-blue pair, with a red and white windmill embroidered on the front.

She was amazing, Rosemary. She also used to have some awesome welts on her arms and her face, that she claimed were a result of her being attacked by her Rottweiler. When we all moved on to high school it got about that her Dad used to beat her up with the jug cord, and then not even any of the boys would go near her, though by that stage she was offering a lot more than a glimpse of her knickers in return for our stares and appreciative sighs.

It was quite nice to have someone like Savy to watch the performance with. After all the other idiots at school he seemed like a decent sort; started telling me about his older sister's awesome music collection that she'd been into since she was eleven. We started to hang out at Sav's place, 'cause his family was the most normal. His Dad was into soccer, (as he told us every time we kicked a ball around), and had even represented the Greater Enderby District as a boy. It was nice to see a forty year old man who wasn't into rugby; something of a rarity in Shackleton. Savy's parents were pretty loose, and not embarrassing like mine were. His Dad was always kind and friendly and would give me and Sav beers to drink if we were having a barbie and would let us smoke cigarettes in front of him, and, all in all, treated me as if I were an adult. Savy's Ma wasn't bad, either. She had some foreign blood in her, from Yugoslavia, or somewhere like that, so she was slightly exotic looking and exciting. His sister was a bit of a pain, but we didn't see that much of her, 'cause she spent most of the time on the phone to her mates, giggling. This was good, 'cause it meant that me and Sav could nick off with her records and play them in the lounge. We found a great place to hide and read Mad Max and Marvel comics, out behind his house in by some bushes. It was good to be able to get away from my home to somewhere decent.

We never hung out at my place. Although Ma had not yet had her first breakdown, she was still prone to calling me "Little Mister" in public, and Dad seemed less and less able to communicate in actual words, and more and more prone to monosyllabic grunts. It was amazing the amount of information he could get across without actually speaking. One short, acknowledging piggy grunt meant "Hi son, how was your day", a lower, more prolonged cow-like moan could be translated as either "I had a shit day" or "Bring me a beer". Usually it meant both. A higher, sharper level of grunt meant "Get the hell out of the house". If I didn't pick up on what Pa's animal language meant quickly enough, I got belted about the face. So I learned to play leave home, stay away from home. I spent more and more time at Savy's and we became quite close mates.

Part of what bonded me and Sav together was a mutual fondness for Rosemary and her lunchtime performances. Anyway, I guess that I really had a couple of mates that year, if you could count a girl as one of them. We all got pretty chummy and eventually the three of us got a bit of a scheme going, whereby me and Savy would act as Rose's guardians and charge boys fifty cents to see Rose lift her skirt up. She was bloody pretty, so most of the guys agreed. They were kind of addicted to the sight of her by this time, anyway.

All the money we made, we split three ways. This seemed fair. After all, Savy and I were Rosemary's protection against fuckwits like Finger. Nobody ever touched her after the word about what Savy had done to Finger got around, although by the end of the year people were getting bored of just seeing undies, so we had to up the stakes a bit. Rose was all for it. She started wearing no knickers at all, and for a dollar, guys could lie prone on the ground and look up her skirt. She was damned tough for her age and I admired her guts. The scheme was brilliant. Rich Loris Knight excluded, we were the wealthiest three kids at the school.

There was a slight hitch in the plan when Savy's parents started getting suspicious about why he had so many comics and cigarettes, 'cause he always blew his money, whereas I stashed mine away in a little tin under my bed with the lunch money I was saving. Savy came up with the idea that we should share a paper round, so as he'd have some sort of explanation for his financial plenitude. I wasn't acquiring any assets so my parents weren't suspicious, but I agreed to do the round just to get some extra money. Rose didn't need to explain nothing to nobody; her Ma was dead, and her father wouldn't have noticed if she'd been earning a grand a week, instead of about ten bucks. She didn't want to do the paper run neither; she had her career and she was sticking to it.

Me and Sav got a nice little job that only covered about a block of the town, though we pretended to Savy's parents that we were delivering to most of Shackleton. With pamphlet delivery as a convenient financial guise our racket with Rose continued on until the end of the year. Then I fell out with the both of them and the whole thing came to a stop.

The three of us were fairly inseparable for a while, even though hanging out with Rose meant that none of the other boys talked to me or Savy apart from when they wanted a perve. But then, they'd never talked much to us anyway, so not a lot had changed. Me and Sav did a bit of girly stuff, just 'cause we both liked Rosemary so much; going to see Madonna in *Desperately Seeking Susan*, listening to Duran Duran and Boy George when maybe we should've been out playing a bit more sport.

As the end of the year grew closer, we made less and less money off Rosemary. Some of the boys started saying that she was getting all up herself and not spreading her legs properly and they couldn't get a worthy view. Somebody suggested that what she had to show was nothing special, and that they might as well go out to their Uncle's farm at the weekend and inspect the sheep. I, also, began to grow a little tired of Rose. Not of the masturbatory image which I held so dear, but of the real Rose. Why should I live with the reality when I could have the fantasy? I had discovered that girls of my imagination were a lot more fun than the girls I knew at school. For a start, none of the girls at school would suck me off, (I had asked a couple), yet the girls of my imagination were more than willing. In fact, they were positively lining up and begging. In comparison to the nubile women of my fantasies, Rose was starting to get boring. She'd recite tedious stories she had made up while blokes were peering up her skirt. In these stories, the heroine was usually a princess of some sort or another.

Sav was usually sucked in by these dumb tales and nicked more and more records for Rosemary from his sister's collection. I began to resent the time that Savy and Rose spent together. Increasingly, they told jokes which were intended to exclude me and giggled about events I had never attended. I also suspected that they were withholding profits from our lunchtime business, but never managed to pluck up the courage to confront them about it. Towards the end of the year I hardly went round to Savy's place at all, 'cause whenever I did, him and Rose'd be playing at some dumb thing, or Sav would be getting Rose to imitate his mother's movements so that she'd be more feminine and business at lunchtime would pick up. I was only earning about a dollar a day off Rose by now and was glad that I had my paper run to fall back on, or I would be hard pressed to afford the increasing number of fags that I was smoking.

Business and friendship both ended one evening when I thought I'd go round to Sav's to try and convince him to come down to the park for a bit of a kick around with a soccer ball. I knocked on his front door, and his Ma answered and said that he'd gone down to the back of the house with some comics. I hadn't known she'd clicked on to our hiding place, but she must've. She looked embarrassed and apologised for the fact that her hair was still all up in rollers. I thanked her anyway, even though she wasn't looking as nice as she usually did, and then I made my way round to where me and Sav used to hide out. I couldn't hear him in there, but the branches at the opening were quite thick and grown over 'cause we hadn't used the hole for a while, so I pushed on through a few more branches and got quite scratched. I could hear some strange noises and thought that it might be Savy's sister and one of her boyfriends in there, so I yelled out 'Oi fuck off!', but the noises kept going, so I thought I might as well keep quiet and go in further for a bit of a perve. There I found Savy and Rose going for it on the ground.

I never liked many people after that.

***

By the time I resurfaced, a lot had happened. My case had appeared before the court and I was found not guilty. Ma had arranged it all, bribed the judge and jury. She'd been there for me when I came round, spouting her words of wisdom. "If only you'd taken my advice and gotten rid of the girl", "That'll teach you to talk back to your old Mum", "So it needed four cell walls to get the message through, eh son." But God! She'd really come through for me this time. The Zepher was waiting on the main road out of Enderby. The boot was loaded up with cans of kerosene and she had even bought me four different coloured lighters; each signifying a differing intensity of flame. Red, orange, yellow, white. On the passenger seat lay four cartons of Marlboroughs - a bribe. That woman could play me like a flute. We would take the road up the coast, all the way to Titan, stopping in at every town, wreaking destruction. The dead were rooting for me.

# EPISODE EIGHT

## *Highway Naught*

We were headed for Titan, the only city that shines brighter than Vegas. The sign on the side of the road said Highway Naught. The road itself dropped down through a sharply cut gorge; cliff rose steeply upwards on either side of the tar seal. The Zepher took the bends like a true dream. The Marlboroughs had fuelled my nicotine addiction nicely. I had smoked half a carton in two days and was beginning to feel like an over-flowing ashtray. Just as I had finished a cigarette, good old Ma would put in an appearance.

"It's time you showed some appreciation for all that I've done for you! Christ knows yours was a rough birth, swear to God you were clinging to my labia on the way out! Even in the womb it was nothing but kick kick kick. And where's the vengeance you're promised to wreak on behalf of me and the old man? We wanna see some flame, little boy, and all we're getting is crisis after crisis. Frankly, we're getting a little tired of waiting for you to get your third-rate act together. We've booked you into a Motel Pteron and it wasn't none too cheap, neither. You're on Highway Naught now, my boy, and it only leads deeper into the heart of nothing. You can see a bit of greenery now, buy you'll get past that soon enough and then you'll be in the stones and from there, just the hard clay roads stretching on and on as far as the eye can see. You have to keep your headlights on, so that the drivers of the cars coming the other way wake up when they see you. That's the way it is, son, that's what you'll be driving through."

"Sure Ma."

"They got rattlers out there, all kinds of crazy wildlife. You never know what's gonna get you."

"Mm-hm."

"So enjoy the green stuff and waterfalls while you can."

"Point taken."

I lit another cigarette. On the third puff I inhaled a little too vehemently and came very close to coughing up both lungs. This was something I wanted to avoid. I needed to keep a hold of all the body parts I could.

"The gift of destruction don't come easy", said Maman. "Be prepared for a little darkness and a little horror."

Famous last words, and she was gone.

\*\*\*

Mawson is a hell of a town to get out of. There are queues of hitchhikers standing on the sides of the road, thumbs out, been waiting there for centuries, legs heavy like lead. Dawson's Motel Pteron sign has a vacant side only. This Pteron was run by a retired Reverend and his disabled wife. She barked orders while he changed her colostomy, wiped the reception counter down with a rotting Kleenex, tightened the springs on the mini-tramp and repainted the Vacant sign.

My room held no disappointments. Purple vinyl sofa, complete with obligatory stains, TV tuned into thirty different stations of static, rotting carpet, jug without an element. I put a pot of water on the stove to boil, sat back in the sofa and watched some static. After a while it became highly entertaining. Pictures moved in shapes of nothingness. A man poured kerosene on a rickety building, a suspiciously shadowy figure moved up and down a set of stairs, a cattery went up in flames. I switched off the set and sat with the cuppa I had made, dunking the tea bag in and out of the milky water, wondering if I was the only guest in Motel Pteron that night. Highly probable. Highly probably that I was the only guest at Motel Pteron that year.

Which made it the perfect target.

I switched out the light in my room and walked over to the window. Rev and Cripple had set themselves up in the reception area. Night vigil. Well, you can't be too careful with all those hitchhiker types just hanging around. I remembered my old mantra - *Douse with the left, light with the right.* Rev and Cripple were nowhere wealthy enough to warrant burning. The only room that needed torching was my own.

The Rev moved over to re-wipe the counter. I grabbed my puffy orange jacket off the sofa, and snuck out to the car for some kerosene. The room would go down. But first, the name of any victim must be writ large. Meticulously, I etched out PTERON on a patch of grass to the rear of the reception building in preparation for later lighting. I went back to the Zephyr, released the handbrake, and pushed the baby 500 metres down the road. It wouldn't be good form to be seen screeching from the place. Far better to fake my own death. Of course! Somebody had come crashing through the doorframe, held a gun to my temples, taken my keys, torched the room and sped off in the Zephyr. Rev and Cripple hadn't required a license plate number. Surely this would be the cleanest crime.

I decided that the vinyl sofa would make good sport and gave it a good thorough dousing. Surely that would be enough to set the whole place blazing. I used the red lighter and lit with my right hand; that right hand that had so elegantly come back from the dead. On the way out I threw more kerosene over the door frame, and walked out through a mouth of blazing light. Lighting the letter P on my way across the lawn, I watched in satisfaction as the word Pteron blazed upon the lawn.

The tranquillity of a job well done.

\*\*\*

I pointed the bonnet towards the bright lights of Titan. Where are you now Mother, to bask in my hard-earned glory? That's the problem with the dead, it's a one way contract. You can weep and you can moan, but they're not about to come down in a shroud of white light if they're not in the mood. Whereas you, you can be having a terrible day, and they can appear any time they want. And they're terrible, every last one of them. Put the fear of God into any man who was in his right mind. I did not ask for this! I never wanted to serve the insatiable appetites of those in the next world. What I wouldn't give to be sitting now, in front of the telly, home-cooked dinner on lap, arm around a good woman, maybe a sprog on the way. Who said I wanted to be pursued down Highway Naught by relentless ghosts? I only ever wanted to be allowed to rest. Mum? Are you listening?

No reply. I am sending dead letters.

I slept in the back of the car and nearly froze to death. Everything was slowing down. The energy that had been whipping me onwards since I left Kensington had dissipated and I was left with a Sunday afternoon feeling of anxiety and ill-ease. So much time on my hands was dangerous. I could sense the seconds hanging heavy in the air, like so many overfed fruit flies. My sense of satisfaction at last nights successful arson had disappeared with that morning's frost, and I was left, once again, chilled to the bone, both literally and metaphorically. None of the berries that the fruit flies gorged on would be mine to pick. Without a companion, either living or dead, I was gutted and hung up to bleed like a carcass in an abattoir.

How much I had packed into the last few months! My time had been a veritable whirlwind of activity, leaving me little if any time for contemplation. And now that I did have time to think, I discovered that thinking was a dangerous past-time. I had no idea of the date. Somewhere in August was all I knew. How long must I wait till spring, till the lilies on the sides of the road shot forth brilliant yellow stamens and the geraniums burst into twelve different shades of red? Patience had never been my strong suit. Titan was not a lighthouse beacon set into a solid piece of rock, but a flickering lamp that moved further away the faster I travelled towards it. All my dreams were turning to ash and dust. I was not the master of disguise I so prided myself on being. Well, I had been caught, hadn't I, and thrown into a cell. Failure weighed in heavy upon me. I was the anti-Midas. Everything I touched just turned to lead. Still, I had not choice. I must go on. I wasn't even into the nothing desert yet, so it must still be a long way to Titan.

As I had at the supermarket, I trilled a little tune in order to cheer and reassure myself. Certainly, I would soon strike another small town worth burning.

## Snuff

The year I got really interested in snuff was my second year at high school. I did not want to hurt anything. I just wanted to have a bit of fun. I suppose you could put it down to boredom if you wanted to. Me I did not want to put it down to anything. I wasn't much interested in child psychology.

I didn't want to watch anybody else's movies, I wanted to make my own. I had a bit of money left over from my paper run and from the business venture Me and Savy'd had with Rose. I never spent my money on anything; I was a right stingy bastard, that was what everybody said; fags were my only expense. Ma had given up on making my lunch at the beginning of Form One and had been giving me two dollars every day since in the expectation that I would buy myself a little something from the cafeteria. We had a fine range of quality food: mince pies, steak and egg pies, steak and mushroom pies, steak and cheese pies, jelly pies, sausage rolls, hot chips and doughnuts. I hated lunch, it always made me feel sick, so every day I just put my two dollars in a little tin I kept under my bed and by the time I got to the third form I had a nice little stash. I liked to look at that money and run it through my fingers and think about what I could buy with it. I was not going to spend it on some stupid thing like Savy'd spend his money on. I was going to buy something big and decent and powerful. Something with potential.

It felt so clean and total; I could feel the power of it pulsing in my palm. I was not holding a video camera, I was holding endless possibilities; the ability to capture and arrange images. I could feel the fullness of the world moving down the lens and into my own eye; the explosion in my hand.

I had not yet become acquainted with vacancy.

The first thing I filmed was just a straight narrative piece about a couple of flies carking it underneath some spray. They crawled about, drugged and terrified for two minutes and fifteen seconds, then the one on the left fell over on its side, emitted one final buzz and was silent. The one on the right replied with a lower, more anaesthetised whine, crawled forward half a centimetre and stopped short in the manner of a clockwork toy or a Grandfather clock that was never to go again. There was a bit of a voice-over; nothing fancy, just yours truly talking briefly about the film's conception, etc, etc.

I felt like God.

That was the first day.

The second day I bought a $20 mixed bag of fireworks and stole five rats, a roll of masking tape and a lab coat from the school's biology lab. The rats were living a death in life anyway; I was just speeding up the process. At this stage it had not occurred to me that what I was about to do might be considered cruel. In general, most things had stopped occurring to me. I hadn't spoken a word to another person in about a week, and, as if to fill the absence, I could hear the voice of my own consciousness trumpeting loudly in my brain. I will buy the fireworks. I will steal the rats. I caught myself speaking silent meaningless words; walking down the street, my lips moving and no sound coming out, no real thought behind the mouth formations. *Rat, rat, rat* was the dull thud of my heartbeat and explosion was the silent sound upon my lips. I was not so into speaking.

   When I got home from school, the house was quiet and empty. The bag on my back was moving and it smelt. I took my haul up to my room and waited until it grew dark and I heard my parents leaving the house to go down to the Suburban Club for a few drinks. I put on the white lab coat in preparation for the festivities, and dragged Ma's old mini-tramp out from her bedroom, through the house and into the back garden. I switched on the back porch light and placed the mini-tramp down upon a grey patch of concrete; a launching pad. It was autumn and everything was dying away into muted shades of green and red. Nothing was in bloom.

This was going to be slightly trickier than the flies.

Withdrawing the largest, whitest, meanest-looking rat from the bag, I placed it right-way-up on the tramp. The springs at the side acted as a convenient moat-like device; basically, the bastard was a goner. I picked up my camera for a bit of pre-apocalypse filming. The framed rat crawled about aimlessly on the canvas. Years of being stuck in the same maze had fooled it into thinking it was clever and knew about escape routes, but placed out in the open it found itself at a complete loss and shuffled about like an old granddad searching for his walking stick. I laughed and shut off the camera. Taking a skyrocket and the masking tape from my bag, I walked over to the rat and grabbed him about the middle.

He didn't struggle much; life as a lab rat at high school had knocked most of the stuffing out of him. I taped the rocket to his stringy tail and re-positioned him on the mini-tramp. He tried to walk a few steps, but seemed to find the rocket too heavy for his person. Eventually he stopped attempting to move altogether, and stood, mid-tramp like a harnessed horse. Old Ninny was about to reach Nirvana. I was glad the skyrocket had a lengthy fuse.

I lit the rocket and a cigarette and ran to take up position behind the lens. Ninny could sense the fire creeping up towards him, yet seemed to have no will to attempt to run from it. This was disappointing. I had always enjoyed a bit of a struggle. I began the countdown. TEN, NINE, EIGHT, SEVEN, SIX, FIVE, FOUR, THREE....FUCK! The rat pre-empted me. Bloody amateurs. Still, it was a sight alright, the rodent shooting off into space; a fiery kite rising and falling in an explosive arc of flame. The rocket and the rat squealed in unison; such music to my ears.

I kept the camera focused on the falling rodent. There was beauty in his fall; such impotent streaming through the empty air. If you squinted your eyes right and put things a bit out of focus, you could pretend that it was flight. The rats still in the bag were making little ratty noises, obviously impatient for a turn in the limelight.

'All good things come to those who wait', I said in reassurance, the first time I had heard my voice aloud in days.

Stunt Rat had no voice-over other than the countdown. I had decided that in this instance, silence conveyed more meaning than sound.

When the rat finally fell from sight, I reached into the squirming bag and withdrew the second largest specimen, also white. Holding him in one hand, I took a Catherine Wheel from my little bag of tricks, stabbed the stem of the firecracker into the ground and taped the rat onto the stem.

Through the extension of my eye, I saw Rat Two freeze rigid with terror, as the world above him spun mercilessly and shot out coloured sparks.

This was beginning to be a drone. I needed some sort of finale, or the film would lack direction and meaning.

I took the remaining three rats from the pack, strapped them together with tape and laid them prone on the tramp. Small ratty feet trod invisible treadmills. I stabbed a sparkler into the stomach of each rat; candles in a birthday cake. I lit the sparklers and filmed the slow bright death; the blood and the sparks and the light.

When all was finished I switched off the porch lamp and walked back inside, leaving the charcoaled corpses half dead upon the tramp. I climbed the stairs to my room, hid the tape in my bottom drawer and lay down on my bed, listening to the thumping of my heart, the narrow evidence of the fact that I was alive, the main valve opening and closing like a fist. Opening and closing and opening and closing and closing around a pebble; a tight grey kernel of pain. A silent cold core of waiting.

It struck me that what I had done might be considered sick.

# EPISODE NINE

*Travelling On*

Poinsett's Motel Pteron was located on the second-floor of a run-down old building that looked as if it had once been a brothel. My customary chat with the man on the desk was pierced intermittently with hisses and yelps to which Mr Receptionist seemed oblivious. The floorboards on which I stood trembled with the noises which rose up from the bottom storey.
"Cattery", I was informed. "There before we were. Time and time again we've tried to get them evicted, but the council won't have a bone of it."
I was shown promptly to my room. I was pleasantly surprised by the decor. No ordinary sofa this, but purple vinyl! And a TV set covered in hard green plastic. All my Christmases had come at once. REOW! I checked out the drinks cupboard. Yep. The customary empty Jim Beam sample bottle. They must get some real desperados staying in places like these. REOW! I walked away, leaving the cupboard door swinging. The medicine cabinet was pretty much the same. A half used can of Gillete shaving foam, a rusty razor blade, a used teabag and a crumbling cake of Palmolive. I opened the door of the fridge and found one gnawed plum pip. It didn't pay to explore within the rooms at Motel Pterons. REOW! All you ever found was other people's half-used shit. Pterons were designed for people who needed somewhere cheap and falling apart and continuously vacant. Those wanting luxury could go to the Sheratons and the Regents. Pterons were designed for those who just wanted to sit back and enjoy the telly.
I perched on the edge of the sofa, switched on the set and absorbed Amazonian Gladiators. REOW CSSSS HISS REOW HISS! Six foot wonders with enormous breasts wrestled each other in a net suspended over an alligator-filled pit. REOW! Christ! What a male fantasy. I put my hand down my pants and sat back into the sofa, wishing that I was an alligator. REOW GRRR HSSSS! The telly was old and did not have a remote, so I was forced to walk the five

metres between the sofa and the set in order to manually turn up the sound and drown out the yelps of the felines.

Across the nation tonight, millions would be watching these women fight. Reow. The thought filled me with wonder, expectation and excitement. I was tuning in to a collective fantasy. hiss. In a way, as a male, I was responsible for these women on the telly. I mean, they were my fantasy. Reow. It was almost as if I had summoned them into being. My heart swelled with pride. Reow. Near my genitals, I had a tentative grope with my right hand. Reowwwwerrrrgrrrhissrr. Good God. All a man asks for is a bit of peace and quiet in order that he may indulge his sexual fantasies and tendencies towards self-aggrandizement, and what does he get but the muted cries of caged animals. I have never been fond of felines, not even those stiff old moggies with the silent meows. This world would be a better place without Felis domesticus. I would do my bit for the cause. Hell, I didn't need a place to sleep. That's what the back seat of the Zephyr was for. The only reason I stayed in these dives was to set them alight. I had to remember my purpose and not succumb to easy comforts.

I snuck out to the car and grabbed some kerosene from the boot. Excellent. What with the Poinsett Pteron being right on top of the cattery, this job was gonna be a double decker. You'd think that the torching of two Pterons in two days would excite the press. The sad thing about the last motel I'd lit was that nobody had even cared. I don't think Mawson even had a local newspaper, and the reporters at the big centres like Enderby and Titan could probably think of nothing less interesting than a motel burning down in a tiny offbeat town like Mawson. However, once the fires at the two Pterons were linked, I had faith that they would run an article on me in every major paper. God, Mum would be proud. Nothing's name printed everywhere. But Titan'd really be the big one, the one that would ensure immortality.

I entered the cattery through a rotting back door. The place stunk of rotting fur, old piss, jelly-meat and inhumanity. I couldn't see any of the animals, nor was there any sign of a mortal. Nervously, I wondered about night watch vigilantes. I felt my stomach retch. The stench was nauseating; poor creatures. They'd struck it lucky with an animal liberationist such as yours truly having stumbled across such cruelty. Release was my middle name.

It was too dark to go in any further and I was on the verge of vomiting. I spread a trail of kerosene from where I was standing to the door, stood in the doorframe and flicked the orange lighter. Hell, what adrenalin. The gulp of the flame and the beating of my own heart in my ears. From deep within the building came the yelping of the burning cats, than a pop and a hiss and the fetid reek of burnt fur. The flames licked higher up the side of the building, engulfing Pteron as planned. I backed away, towards the Zephyr. A burning animal shot out of a nearby window, and landed, eyes wide, still breathing at my feet, fur shooting from its sizzling body in small, tidy clumps. I screamed in horror and satisfaction, then leapt into the front seat of the Zephyr.

The hum of the engine.

## *Plaster casts*

School continued to provide a steady supply of rodents and an even steadier supply of boredom. When my $20 mixed bag of crackers ran out, I knew it was time to turn my hand to something a little more solid. I had begun to enjoy stealing for the first time since the Obadiah incident and often took supplies from the art room in return for the $150 my parents paid in school fees each year. Under my bed, along with the emptied money tin, I kept a nice lot of provisions: watercolours, oils, pastels, crayons, inks, dyes, varnish, gloss, several types of brush, plenty of quality paper, a large bag of Plaster of Paris and several rubber moulds. What with all that behind me, I knew I would be able to whip up something a little special for my next set of volunteers.

I gave them names: Daisy, Candy, Horace, Bill, Bill. It seemed to make it more personal, as if we had a real connection; that unique bond between scientist and specimen. I treated these babies nicely; brought them home, made them a little house from an old cardboard box, put some straw in there for them to nestle in. I even went down to the toy store and purchased a miniature plastic TV and radio so as they would not get too bored.

All the comforts of the middle class.

I gave them a week or so to get settled in. Thursdays my parents always went out to the Suburban Club, so that night I skipped dinner and sat anxiously up in my room, waiting for the noises that signified my parent's departure. As soon as I heard the car doors slam, I ran down to the bathroom with the box of rats under my arm, and set up the camera so that it focused on the bathroom bench. I got a bright red plastic bowl from the kitchen and mixed some of the Plaster of Paris up with a bit of water. I took the first yellow rubber mould, which was of Snow White, and I dusted her insides with talc, so as nothing would stick to her. I poured a smidgen of plaster inside, and then I picked up Candy by the tail and plonked her in nose first. She started to protest and squirm about a bit, but I soon rectified that with another good dose of plaster. The mould was a lot bigger than she was, so pretty soon she was just upside down swimming in a pool of sticky plaster. I pulled the bottom of Snow White's dress up around the tail of the rat and put a rubber band around, so that the tail stuck out through the yellow mould. That way I could have a gauge of the rat's mental state. Recording the time of Operations Complete, I placed the whole contraption in the bathroom sink and began on the second rat.

The next mould I used was the bust of a garden gnome; a short, stumpy, ugly, warty thing, with very few redeeming features and no legs. I prepared the mould in the same way that I had for Candy, then I picked up Bill, stuck him in head first and quickly covered him over with plaster. I had liked this one the least; he was quite spineless and by far and away the most unintelligent of all the rats I had stolen. Even when he was completely covered up with the plaster, he was still trying to turn around in the mould, and kept stretching his head against the side of the rubber, not realising he was done like a dog's dinner. I laughed, and squeezed my hands tightly around his neck, listening to him choke. In my palms, I could hear his tiny ratty heart beating faster and faster. Then I felt it cease altogether. Just in case, I tied the bottom of the mould as I had with Snow White and placed Bill down beside Candy in the sink. I was pleased to note that Candy's tail had stopped twitching.

I turned around, smiled, and did a peace sign to the camera.

I finished off the other three rats in this way, and then I put them back in their little box and carried them up the stairs to my room. I went back down to the bathroom, switched off the camera and cleaned up. It would not matter if Ma and Pa came home now, 'cause that was far and away the worst part over and done with.

I lay on the floor of the lounge and watched telly for a couple of hours, every now and then going up to check on rodent progress. I had to be dead careful that Ma and Pa did not catch me. Last time I had been stupid and careless and Ma had come home to find a trio of barbequed rats on her mini-tramp, sparkler stems still sticking up out of their little bellies. I'd had to blame it on the next-door-neighbour's boy; ten year old Seamus. When confronted by both my mother and his own, Seamus had denied everything; but it was my word against his, and I was the elder and more sensible of the two. Seamus was now seeing a child psychiatrist, and this pleased me infinitely, although at some level I was jealous. A psychiatrist sounded like great sport to me, when I though of what fabulous tales I could make up for my own amusement. But it was Seamus who was having his head read, and I who was here, free, watching telly and waiting for my rats in plaster to dry.

My parents came home, drunk and obnoxious, and I retired to my room with three glasses of water, claiming excessive thirst. By this time Candy and Bill were well set. I shook them from their moulds and contemplated my lovely range of art supplies.

*And Candy looks lovely tonight in a flowing gown of yellow and black, teamed with a delicate mother of pearl necklace. Unfortunately, Candy is wearing no shoes, possibly due to the fact that she has no feet. Bill is decked out in his best gnome wear; a wonderful green pointed hat and a purple jerkin. And our commiserations go out to Bill who lost his legs recently in a fatal accident involving a lawnmower.*

We played fashion games all night. The camera got the whole show. It was great to have some company. When we were all tired out I put my friends up on the shelf by the cuckoo clock and lay in the middle of the floor staring at the daddy long legs which crawled towards a crack in one corner of the ceiling.

From the bottom of the stairs, a drunken mother yelled that it was time for me to switch out my light.

It was nice to know that I was just your average fourteen year old boy.

### *Cast in Stone*

Because I could not find another Pteron to stay in (and torch) I parked the Zephyr on the side of the road near a beach. I spent a rough night sleeping in the back of the car and when dawn crept in I got out from behind the driving wheel and walked down to the beach. The muddy beach was populated with statues; stone men and women frozen in a variety of different poses. The statues all had one thing in common – they were all looking back over their shoulders. I began to walk along the beach. There was a shrieking in the wind; it sounded like somebody standing behind me and calling my name. I turned to look and became stone myself.

How the hell was I meant to get out of this one?! My limbs felt as heavy as lead; no body part would move although I was doing my best to send commands from my brain to my limbs. I was stuck, trapped; a fly caught in amber. Just as I had resigned myself to my fate, who should come swooping in from across the ocean but my good old Ma. Two gigantic white wings sprouted from her shoulders. She was furious with me.
'What the hell kind of scrape have you got yourself into now?' she asked me.
I couldn't reply, so I didn't. She tut-tutted for a bit and then swooped me up in her arms and flew out to sea with me. She dropped me from a great height. I fell into the sea with a splash and began to melt. The sea was dissolving me! The stone cast I had been locked up in cracked and opened up and I fell out, glad to be free, glad to be human. Dead people do have some uses then.

***

Drowning was nice. Straight from one form of death to another, feeling the pressure of the water closing in over my head; stillness and silence. My past didn't flash before my eyes as promised, but I guess that was due to the fact that my life had been pretty embarrassing and God wanted to save me from any unnecessary humiliation. Looking up, I could see Maman screaming and swooping above the surface of the ocean, but could no longer hear her words. I was not drowning, but nor was I swimming.

I began to become embryonic; a little piggy fish, gills and all. My skin became foetal tissue, and I thought of Keith in his freezing drown. Is this what he had experienced? It wasn't at all unpleasant, this type of metamorphosis. That little boy had been damn lucky that I had decided upon the partially thawed lake for that skating trip. Thanks to me he had experienced something pure and terrible and rare. I had sent him, from life, back through birth to Nirvana. What a trip! I, also, liked to travel. Long live the unborn. A whooping laugh escaped my lips. Surely it was a blessing to play Lazarus three times in such a short space. Back from burning, back from stone, and now acting the embryo. My skin glowed with a yellow translucence, my whole being an aureole. In such a state, being eaten away by light, I hummed. What else could I do? I'd left Mama far behind, and my fate was now in my own vacant hands. Sinking changed to floating and I bobbed about quite happily, content with my lot. Fortune had dealt me a winning hand; thanks old girl. Of course, I could not foresee how this latest death by drowning would turn out. Third time unlucky?

The quiet ascension began; the slow drift skywards. The water streamed past the milky albumen of my skin, filtering through my gills, giving me breath underwater. I flapped like white flannel, drifting upwards, twisting, waving, turning; free of any umbilical noose.

The comfort began to scare me. I had deceived myself; my fate was not in my own hands and it never had been. There was nothing pleasant about drowning. I started to panic and found I couldn't breathe. I was becoming human and could hear my mother and some mermaids singing.

The more I struggled for my breath, the more I choked. My fishy gills became water-filled lungs and I rose to the surface, spluttering and dead. Mum stood on the shore applauding as I lay face down at her feet; my hair flowing from my skull and spreading out across the watery mud.

# EPISODE TEN

## *Re-birth*

She was human again, but I was not. I was halfway; Lazarus without the comeback. I made a couple of attempts; a motor starting, spluttering, and falling silent. Mama, resplendent in a flowing green gown and red spikey high heels, jumped up and down on my back in     an     attempt     to     revive     her     only     son.
"We're counting on you, come back! Come back!"
Same old stuck record. Well I was sick of it. Sick of the whole damn shebang.

I looked down from above, as she had looked down at me, so many times, just swooping in with instructions and messages from the dead. Why should I make my return? She didn't need me to carry out services on behalf of those in the next world, she just needed somebody. Any old sucker could do the job. If I left this world behind she would be forced to find another to carry out her shitty missions of vengeance. And, just as I had ascended through the ocean, so I began to ascend through the air. I'd done my time, it was appropriate that I now left this planet far behind me. I hovered on the border.

And then I thought of the person who would come next; that poor stupid bastard whom Momma would surely pick on should I chose to absent myself from the picture. I remembered all that I had been through; I wouldn't wish the cumulative sequence of events of the last three months on my own worst enemy, let alone a fellow avenger. And I was so far in now; I had to finish the job. I could see Titan ahead of me, the lights of the city shimmering; the last stop on this fugue of fire. I deserved the reward of seeing a major city burn at my own hand. After all, I had paid and paid; and it seemed to me that the dead winter growth had seen the fruition of some nice new sprouts. There had been two Pterons and a cattery, hadn't there? I was only being tested so that I might build up new strength. This was the way it ran with me; disaster always producing new energy. I attracted catastrophe like the South Pole attracted

**84**

magnets with a Northern current. Apocalypse was sent from above; from Mother and from Father, those two puppet-masters so bent on control.

Momma had kicked off the red stilettos and was down on her knees in the mud, attempting to give me the kiss of life. I watched her breathing into the mouth of the deflated doll which now lay on its back in the shallows of the water, watched her pumping her hands up and down above the heart which had once beat as steadily as a two-bob watch. As I lay dying, history was happening without me.

Still I hung; undecided, then began to rise, higher, away from the floppy form which lay before my mother, lifeless. It was getting hard to breathe. Things grew paler.

Then they materialized; my deciding factor.

The pearly gates. A petite Saint Pete stood on guard, wearing a creamy polyester Safari Suit, grasping the Book of Life in one hand and a Bo-Peep crook in the other and looking suspiciously like a figure from a pop-up cardboard Bible book. Pete was very small and very messy. The Safari Suit was open to the waist, exposing an anaemic looking torso and some sharply defined ribs. His hair hung down in clumps about his grimy-looking face and he smelt like an old fish factory. I was disappointed. What was more, the pearly gates were not pearly at all, but made of a cheap wrought-iron and decorated with crudely wrought Gorgons, one of which opened her jaws wide and snarled at me as I approached. No blazing candles, no gold-plating, no throne with a lamb on it. I doubt they even had a lamb up here; it was all a big bloody con.

All in all, I felt pretty ripped off by the whole thing. I swayed before Pete who then extended a forefinger and tapped a black nail against the leather bound cover of the book which contained the names of the most elitist club ever to exist in history. The nail of the tapping finger was blackened, not by courtesy of any expensive polish or slamming door, but by a marker pen. I knew this, because Pete, after tapping, took the pen out of his pocket and began colouring in the remainder of his nails, idling, my future in his hands.
"Name?" barked the Safari Saint.

"Nobody."

"Right then."

He put the pen between the jaws of the nearest Gorgon and consulted the notorious book.

"Nehemiah, Noah......Noddy. Sorry. No can do."

I hated old Pete then, with a hatred as pure and sharp and cold as steel. Not only was there no justice in the world, but there was no justice in heaven, either. Then I remembered - it's not what you've done, it's who you know.

"What about my father? He's in there somewhere. He'll give you a character                                                                                   reference."

"What's                                   his                                   name?"

"Father Nobody."

"Oh.......Father Nobody. I think you want purgatory. That's that way."

He pointed straight down.

"Dad's                                   in                                   hell?"

"Limbo."

Grief ran through me like an electric jolt.

"But he never did anything wrong."

"Exactly. And he never did anything right either. You think getting a few electric cables to the right people at the right time qualifies him for entry? Think again little boy. It takes something a bit special    to    get    in    through    these    gates."

He patted the wrought iron.

"He's waiting for you to prove yourself. Don't make him wait forever!"

He pushed an ebony nail hard into the middle of my forehead, and drew blood.

"Identification tag", said Pete. "When you come here again, there'll be no need for explanation."

A gorgon snarled and I was shooting downwards; a skyrocket in reverse.

## Fay's Big Catch

I once attacked a henhouse. I was pretty messed up at the time, 'cause I'd just broken up with the only girlfriend I've ever had, on account of the fact that she refused to have an abortion. This was when I was about sixteen, before the thought of turning to arson as a constructive method of channelling my emotions had even crossed my mind. Back then I still talked to a few people even if I didn't really like them all that much. I don't feel proud of what I did. In hindsight, I can see that I should never have taken it out on those helpless chooks. It was largely the thought of impending fatherhood that did it. It can't have been the break up 'cause I didn't even like the girl that much. I only went out with her 'cause I wanted something to shag, and, except for Rose, most of the women in Shackleton wouldn'tve touched me with a ninety-foot barge pole. You couldn't have a one night stand, either, in a place like Shackles, 'cause everyone knew who you were and if you were repulsive like me, no-one wanted to get it on with you in case you turned psycho.

So I had to convince Fay to go out with me, else I was going to remain a virgin till I was a hundred and eight. She only went out with me, 'cause no-one else had been interested in her for a while. Her parents told her they thought I was a creepy pervert and that I couldn't stay the night (even though all her past boyfriends had been allowed to). So we usually had to do it standing up in the public toilets, (she always made me go into the women's), or lying down in some of the shrubs at the botanic gardens. We weren't really that involved, and hardly ever even talked to each other.

I hadn't been inside her head, I'd only been inside her body.

More than anything, I couldn't stand the unfairness of it all. There were blokes at my school who'd been shagging since they were thirteen or fourteen and they'd never got anyone pregnant, and here's me having managed (against all the odds) to get a shag at sixteen and most of the time practising come-on-the-leg contraception and still the woman gets pregnant. It was all her fault. If I'd known she was so excessively fertile, I never would've shagged her in the first place. I'd been had! She couldn't even manage to tell me about the baby to my face, which I'd thought was pretty wimpy of her. She told me over the phone. My mouth hung open in shock. We'd only been going out for four months, and, due to the difficult circumstances, we couldn't have done it more than about ten or eleven times. Most of these had ended with me spoofing on her leg, having failed to get it in on time. So I guess we'd had about three times where she might've got pregnant from it, which isn't many, though I suppose it is enough. I was really pissed off with Fay for wanting to stuff up her future by not having an abortion. I'd offered to pay and everything, but she said that wasn't the point, though she couldn't tell me what the point was.

If I recall rightly, the day that I attacked the henhouse, she'd dragged me along to the obstetrician at Shackleton State Hospital and he'd rubbed jelly on her stomach and put some bloody gadget over her where he thought the baby should be. We'd watched the little piggy fish on the screen, twisting and turning and performing small acts of water ballet (show-off!) and I was sure I saw it waving to me with a tiny, marginally formed limb. I felt slightly ill. God knows I wasn't made to reproduce. If the poor bastard was cursed like me and the rest of my family, I would never forgive myself.

I don't want anybody to think I was at all emotionally unstable at this time. I just didn't want to see that poor little foetus come into this world with half of my repulsive looks and half of my grotesque brain. I rung up Fay and offered to give her two hundred dollars on top of the abortion money. On the other end of the line she was crying and swearing at me and telling me I was a stupid asshole. I told her I wished that I was the one who was pregnant, 'cause then I could've done what I wanted to do to that ugly little amphibian, which was to terminate its life right then and there. I said I couldn't believe she wasn't doing what I was telling her to; who the hell did she think she was anyway, to go on and get herself up shit creek when I was going to be the one who'd have to do the financial paddling.

Things got worse. She stopped calling me a stupid asshole and got her father on the phone and he had a good rant at me about how I was a stupid shit who'd stick his prick into anything that moved (a lie - his daughter was the first moving thing I'd stuck it to) and that

I'd 'better bloody well marry her or my name would be Mud'. That last part really cracked me up. As if I would be worried what a bunch of small town inbreds really thought of me. I said I wouldn't marry his daft daughter if she was the last woman left after the apocalypse and he said that he'd see to it that once I left school, I would 'never be able to work in this town again not even a paper run.' I said, 'Well thank you very much Alfred Hitchcock, but I don't intend to stay in this town or marry your daughter so you can just RACK OFF!'

And then he changed the tune he was whistling and got all soft and soppy on me, like he thought that if he greased me up he'd get his way.

'We know you're a nice boy, really, and me and the wife could fix you up alright, give you a little down payment on a place...'

*I'M ONLY SIXTEEN!*

'...and some of Fay's old gear that we've kept all these years just in case something unplanned like this happened...'

*I'VE GOT MY WHOLE LIFE AHEAD OF ME (AND OTHER CLICHES) WHY DON'T YOU ABORT THAT FISHY FOETUS INSTEAD OF MY FUTURE*

'....hello dear...'

They'd put Fay's mother on the phone, the biggest faker out.

'...we're so happy for you...'

*BUT YOU HATE ME, YOU'VE ALWAYS HATED ME.*

'...why don't you come around so we can have a cuppa and talk things through...'

I knew I had to take some serious action. They had to know the real me; they had to meet the killer inside. They could not make me marry their pimply daughter. I had to prove to them that I was not under any circumstances to be mistaken for son-in-law material. I was not the marrying kind and never would be. I went down to the garage and got Pa's axe. The head of it was very blunt but I knew that it would do the trick. I raced back upstairs and raided Ma's underwear drawer for some black pantyhose, but I could not find anything decent and had to make do with a pair of fishnets that smelt as if they needed a wash. I pulled the fishnets down over my face and walked out of the house with the blunt axe swung up over my left shoulder.

All the time I was thinking of the foetus and its tiny limbs. Fay had passed out on the back porch, her mother was screaming her head off and her father was puffing at his cigarette like he was a deep-sea diver and the smoke was his oxygen tank. I was having a great old time, just smashing the axe into the coop and watching the wood splinter and the mesh fall away and the chickens run about squawking and imagining that I could stop the life of that stupid glorified larva. I made a mad dive for a nearby chook and walloped the blade into its neck. Blood gushed out and up over my hands. Fay's mother stopped yelling and began whimpering. I turned to face her, and snarled through my Ma's fishnets.
-*Grrrr*, I said, like the mad ax-wielding maniac that I was. -*Grrr, grrr, grrr.*
The tears were gushing down her face.
-*Grrr*, I said again, and made a lunge at another hen. I got that one also, and then another couple and then another two or three after that. I wanted them to know that it was not safe for me to marry into their family. Nor was it safe for Fay to give birth to something I had sired. I yanked some feathers out of a chook which was running around with its head bloodied but still attached to its body, ripped a hole in the fishnets and stuffed the feathers into my mouth. Blood was trickling down my chin. I was the mad fox got into the henhouse. There was no stopping me.

Now that he'd got more into the swing of things, Fay's Pa looked like he was beginning to enjoy the show. That was the last thing we wanted. I dropped the axe, caught the hen I had stolen the feathers from, and began waving it round above my head. It was still very much alive and was giving out the odd squawk. I spat the feathers from my mouth and began to sing.
-*Why are there so many songs about rainbows and what's on the other....*
I let the chicken fly out and away from me. It hit Fay's dad square in the jay, knocking him back against the faded weatherboards of the house.

*-....side....rainbows are something and something la de something and rainbows have nothing to....*
I picked up my ax and began to head towards Fay's prone form.
*hide....someday you'll find it......*
I slammed the blade into the wood of the porch.
*....the rainbow connection, the lovers, the dreamers and...*
Fay's mother came to her senses, grabbed her daughter by the ankles and dragged her past the fly screen and into the safety of the house. I stood there on the porch, face to face with her father, who was now beginning to recover from being hit by a chook.
*-Grrr*, I said, and raised the axe high above my shoulder.
*-You're sick son,* said Dad.
Then he shook his head, slowly, three times and followed his wife into the house.
That night, at home, I tried repeatedly to wash the blood from my hands, but no matter how hard I tried my hands stayed pink and the water grew red.

I dreamt I was hooked underwater, twisting and turning and yanked to the surface. All laid out and sliced down the backbone.

\*\*\*

I didn't see Fay for a couple of weeks, and then she turned up at school. I passed her on the top field, but she just put her head down and walked straight past me. I put my head down also, and saw my red hands.

The word about town was that her parents had forced her to have an abortion. I thought of that little fish and my behaviour with the chooks and I felt embarrassed and guilty. But what options had I really had? I was like a wild animal that behaved nicely enough when it was left alone, but, when cornered, could get very vicious and snarly.

That afternoon, Fay and I had a science class together. Towards the end of the period she came up to me and tapped me on the shoulder and handed me that tiny frog in a jar. It was looking out at me, furled; pressing its forehead to the pane. I stared and stared.

She never spoke to me again.

# EPISODE ELEVEN

*Back*

When I came to, I was kissing my mother. I choked, coughed and spat into her mouth. She swallowed, lovingly, as only the most dedicated of women will do. I fondled the nail mark in the middle of my forehead. Had not St. Pete said *when* you come here again? No doubt about it. Also, I knew that Momma had been telling tales about having descended from heaven. She'd been with Dad, in limbo, all along. Her motives were entirely selfish. She was depending on me to get her out of no-man's land and into Elysian fields. Suddenly, I was no longer her pawn, her puppet, her helpless servant. I had sweet Mama in check and it was soon to be mate.

I knew there was no justice in the world. Freaks lost. That was the bottom line. I was aware of the statistics. But I also knew that I now had the option of playing Mother's keeper. It would be an act in which we both partook. I had once been her faithful pet, but she was soon to become my squalling trapped animal. Relations could be the deadliest of enemies.

I emitted a small whimper and played the victim with consummate skill.

"Look what you've done to me."

She melted as expected.

"Oh my baby boy! I never meant for this to happen. I know that I may have bullied you in the past, but..."

"I never wanted to be an arsonist, Mum..."

An outright lie.

"You kept pushing me. I didn't know how to say no. And then you dropped me Ma, from a very great height."

I winced and grabbed my kneecap, playing her like a piano.

"You've hurt yourself in the fall?"

"Worse than anything the IRA could've done."

"I'm not your enemy, boy. Don't think that I'm against you."

But she had been and she was. At that moment, I blamed her for everything. Why had I been to hell? For her; on behalf of the dead, and also, perhaps, the living.

"Why should I go on burning, Ma?"

She knew the answer. So she and Dad could hot-foot it out of purgatory. She stalled for a more convincing reason, and the old bully-self made a fresh appearance.

"What else can you do? You left the chef's course, nannying saw you kill one of your charges. But pyromania's the game where the biggest loser wins. It's the only thing for you."

The old reptilian wheedling. I made a quick move to the defence.

"Come on. There's lots I can do. For a start..."

I shuffled rapidly through the brain's back files.

"For a start..."

*Blankety blank blank blank blank.*

"I can go on the dole."

I advanced a pawn one square. She took the pawn with a knight.

"Oh come on. You'd be a heroin addict within the week, you know you would. You'd sit around the house, watching the soaps."

"Runs in the family."

I took the knight with a bishop.

"There's nothing else you can do. God! You can hardly even cook and clean for yourself! Arson is your raisin detre..."

"My                                                                        what?"

"Raisin detre."

"Is that the awful dessert you used to make?"

She ignored me, and went on, advancing her queen.

"Think of your old Pa watching on from above."

She wasn't watching the game. I took her queen with a seemingly innocuous pawn which she had overlooked.

"If he's looking on from anywhere, then it's up through layers of molten lava."

She gasped and moved no chess pieces.

"What?"

"Saint Pete's revealed all Ma. You and Dad are both locked out till I get the family name into the book. So I guess you're a little dependent on me, aren't you Mother, having done no good deeds in your own lifetime, and in fact failing to take granny meals when you knew she couldn't fend for herself any longer. You could have been had for neglect."

My mother was the Wicked Witch of the West, melting down into a puddle of green liquid steam. She pointed a feeble finger towards a pawn. I knew that I had her tamed.

"Don't let your old man down."

But what had the old man ever done for me? Or for Ma either, for that matter? The only things I'd ever got out of him had been through blackmail, and this life after death bargaining would be no exception. If I was going to get them both through the gates and into the land of eternal life then they were going to have to come up with something pretty bloody special. I knew Highway Naught cut right through the heart of the desert. It wasn't going to be easy. All in all, there was no point relying on Dad. It was Mum that would be in a position to arrange things. A few desert mirages when I got a bit bored, a couple of conveniently placed oases.

Dad could just hang around and be useless. Ma had always been a woman of action, even if that action was breaking down. And she would do as I wished now; I had gained a new power. My father was a hopeless case, the kind of man who had sat back and watched his life passing by as if he were locked into a cinema, sitting through a fairly tedious film. And now he was content to sit back and watch his death, whilst I took over control of the whole lot; life after death and death in life. Nothing ever changed.

## Blade

Things were pretty rough after I broke up with Fay. I got bored and had to start talking to more people, going out and drinking. This was a year or two before Ma had her first really bad turn, and I was sometimes quite happy. Rose was a regular figure at the parties I went to; usually drunk and passed out on a sofa with her legs spread. She had a penchant for short red plastic skirts which an Uncle who lived in the States used to send over and she wore a lot of cheap light blue eye makeup. She had discovered bleach in the third form, and was now into it in a big way; her hair was always yellow and stringy and breaking off. In a bigoted place like Shackleton all this added up to two words – bloody whore.

The label was a bit of a joke, really, because although everyone said she was an easy lay, none of the guys would go near her, 'cause she had so many bruises from her Pa. Occasionally you'd hear of someone who'd given her a bang in a spare room at a party somewhere, but afterwards he'd always say how drunk he was, or he never would've gone with a loose woman like that. As far as I could see, her reputation as a whore was pretty undeserved, 'cause most of the blokes were too embarrassed to shag her. She might've dressed like a tart, but it don't think it was possible that she could've actually acted like one, unless everyone was having sex with her and then denying it. Perhaps this was what was happening, but I never saw her disappearing with anybody.

Despite the bruises and the layers of make-up, I still thought she was quite beautiful. I did not understand why everyone wanted to avoid her and no-one would give her any help. I couldn't deal with the way that she was nobody's responsibility; that everyone (including myself) turned a continual blind eye to the abuse that was so obviously inflicted upon her on a regular basis. It was as if she had a disease we were afraid to catch. Perhaps it was called alcoholism, 'cause she could polish off a large bottle of most things you would care to name, and even though she'd usually flaked it by the end of the evening, I never once saw her vomit. It was great sport, watching her get drunk and lose all inhibition and try to dance around the room like she did it for a living; skinny spider limbs flailing out in all directions. She had some scary looking knife scars down her arms and her legs, but nobody knew if they'd been done by her or her Pa. I never saw any guys paying her much attention and I was shy about talking to her, 'cause of the incident with Savy when we were kids. I talked to lots of the other girls though, but I never talked to any of the guys.

They were all rugby meatheads, with rubbish taste in music. Someone would always stick on AC/DC and they'd yell out "THUNDER" at random intervals and then someone else would go and get into his school uniform and pretend to be Angus Young. It was pretty funny. When they got bored they'd pull up each others shorts, shout 'HOMO' a couple of times and keep drinking. This was why I hadn't been to any parties before the breakup with Fay.

I soon learnt to assert myself at these gatherings. One night in particular, I'd made some attempts to put on what I was listening to back then, which was Bleach and they'd all started yelling at me and then some bastard had got my CD and snapped it in half. His mates stood round and cheered. I would've killed him, but I only weighed 58 kilos, and he weighed 115. Rose stopped dancing. Everyone started yelling out for Meatloaf.

The beefcake's name was Tanker and he was a prop on the first fifteen. He was having his second time round in the seventh form so that he could have access to the free gym equipment. He spent his whole life in the sawdust pit, but no teacher ever nagged him about it. He was the school's main source of pride. Most people stayed out of his way since he'd gotten into a fight with one of his mates and ended up biting the guy's nose off, but I wasn't gonna let no-one get away with snapping Bleach. After Tanker snapped my CD, Rose came across and said she was sorry about what had happened and she gave me a swig of her 'fill your own' vodka. I said it was not her fault and she needn't worry about it. I reminded her about the lab rat I had stabbed back at Intermediate, but I don't think it really registered with her what I was on about, so I took the blade out of my inside pocket and showed her the edge. It was real sharp and Rose showed the acceptable level of appreciation.

I could not handle anybody breaking my CDs. Anything else would not have mattered to me. I wouldn't have cared if they'd ripped the arms off my leather jacket or torn up some of my favourite

**97**

books, but I could not put up with Tanker snapping my CD and his mates cheering and putting on Meatloaf. I had to re-establish the reputation as a psycho that had kept me safe until now, or I was done for. Let them break one CD and the next thing you know, they'll be in there doing damage to your whole collection. A small bugger like me was at a terrible disadvantage, physically. My razor was only a little thing, more like a scalpel, really, but it was dead sharp and the only sort of weapon I could get my hands on in Shackleton. I did not really want to hurt anyone; it was just for my own self-protection.

I didn't want to make a big thing about it either, and have them all staring at me, so I waited till most of the meatheads had gone outside to where the keg was and it was just me and Rose and Tanker and a few other girls who weren't so bad. Tanker had his back turned to me and was making the moves on this short brunette girl who was a netballer, and she was sort of wincing and looking pained at having to talk to him. I grabbed Rose's arm like we were leaving together and with my other hand I held my razor tight. Tanker hadn't even noticed us moving. I pushed Rose out the door ahead of me and as I passed Tank, I reached up and sliced into the back of his neck, as easily as if it were a Scotch fillet. He yelped twice and then began to whimper like a puppy. For all his beef, he was a soft bloody bastard. Blood was pissing down the back of his neck. I was more than satisfied. As I stepped through the doorway, I waved my blade at him and smiled.

He must've been too embarrassed to tell anyone what'd happened, because I never heard anything more about it and he never hassled me again. From then on I was allowed to put on bits of my own music. When I moved to put a CD on the stereo I always kept one hand in my pocket so that they knew I had a firm grasp of my razor and was not to be messed with. I could not get away with more than every second song, so it would alternate Metallica, Sonic Youth, Iron Maiden, Nick Cave, Slayer, Throwing Muses, White Snake, The Verlaines, Pantera.

The night that I sliced Tanker, I walked Rose home past the botanical gardens where I used to screw Fay. She didn't try to talk to me, which was a good thing, 'cause I wasn't feeling up to much, conversation wise. It was nice just to walk along, a comfortable silence between us. She wasn't one of those dumb girls that have to fill in every gap or pause with a nervous giggle or a stupid anecdote. We didn't talk about Savy. We didn't really talk about anything. She was just quiet, and every so often would quench her thirst with the half-full vodka bottle. Most girls wouldn't have even been able to walk if they'd got so much in them, but Rose had to drink that just to get normal. The highlight of the evening occurred when we swapped phone numbers; it wasn't sexual or romantic, it was just friends.

When we got to her house the light in the main room was on. I could hear her father in there ranting to himself and I was scared for what was going to happen. But she put her hand on my shoulder and reassured me that it would be alright, so I left her to go inside and I went on down the road. When I turned to look back I saw that she was standing in the doorway, watching me walking away. I waved, but she can't have seen me, for she didn't respond, only turned on her heels and went in through the door.

The next time I saw her she was wearing her sunglasses even though it was raining. She'd had a couple of days off school. She was very quiet. Her hair was tied back off her face. I said *are you going to the party tonight?* and she said *na.* Like I said, she wasn't much for conversation.

## EPISODE TWELVE

### *Lilies*

The following day she was off school and I was dead worried. I thought he might have killed her or anything, well you just don't know. I sat at home that evening, listening to my music, and every time the phone rang I jumped right out of my skin but it was never her it was always someone selling Pa some electrical stuff, or Aunty Susan wanting Ma, or some old family friend from Titan wanting to stay on the line for three hours to chat to each one of us in turn. I tried to sleep but I couldn't, so mostly I just paced the room and thought about her bruises.

Around two in the morning it started getting a bit ridiculous, so I decided to go for a walk, like I usually do when sleeping's a dead end street and there's still a lot of hours to go until it's time to wake up. I tried my hardest not to, but I found myself walking past her house. The same light was on in the same room and I could hear a lot of yelling. I didn't know what to do. I went down by the ocean and I watched the boats coming in, the lights glittering across the harbour. I tried to think of nothing, but I couldn't. I could only think of her.

I think about a week must have passed and I had no eyes at all 'cause they never seemed to close; I never got any sleep. I went down to the florist in town and got a bunch of those beautiful Arum lilies, the big open white ones with the bright yellow stamens and I went around to visit. Her Pa came to the door when I knocked and I hid the flowers behind my back. He was only a small bastard but his eyes were hard and twitchy, like a bird's. He stepped aside to let me in and told me where I could find his daughter. I walked down the corridor and up the stairs to Rose's room. She was looking pretty disgusting; her hair hanging down in her eyes and her mouth all purple and swollen up in one corner. At school, Tanker was making jokes about her and saying that she must've jumped on a boat with a bunch of Russian sailors and other funny stuff like that.

I took the Arum lilies out from behind my back and passed them to her and she just said thanks and put them down on the blanket and she didn't even look at them properly to see what I had slipped in under the wrapping. I didn't really have anything to say, 'cause given the circumstances, *how are you?* seemed a bit ridiculous but I just wanted her to know that I'd been thinking about her and how she'd been and all of that. She asked me how was school and I said that it was shit I was just into my music and she said yea I know. I said when are you coming back and she said when I bloody well feel like it so I thought I'd best change the subject but before I could think of what to change it to her Dad was outside bashing on the door and telling me I'd better leave he didn't want nobody getting his daughter pregnant. This was very unfair. I hadn't even been sitting on the end of her bed, I'd just been standing. I kissed Rose on the cheek and left the room.

I lay on my bed at home and thought of the blade among the lilies.

\*\*\*

Well she found it and she must've used it, 'cause I got a call at about midnight saying that I'd better come round quite quickly so I did and she had blood all over her hands like I'd all over mine with those chooks and I couldn't see her father anywhere. Then she led me up some stairs to the attic and there were specks on the way up and he was there on the floor with marks in him like gills only he wasn't breathing through them. She said you never should've given me that and I said I didn't want him to get you again and somebody was bashing on the door downstairs and it was as though we were a movie but we weren't 'cause we were living it. I went down the stairs again, past the specks of red and I answered the door it was a neighbour saying they'd heard something just making sure it was all ok and I said yes it was and I went up back the stairs but they didn't believe what I was saying 'cause next thing there's a knock again and one of those boys in blue. They found her on the floor next to her Pa, crying and they walked her down past me.

And I never saw her again

101

## Desert

Now that I had my mother tamed, there would be no limit to my powers of destruction. The dead were no longer driving me; I was driving the dead. Momma had promised to assume human form until such time as we made it through the desert. I knew this would be the roughest part of the trip. After we had passed through the heart of nowhere, there would be only a few small towns and patches of greenery until we hit the flickering lights of Titan. On the other side of the desert, Ma would be free to leave. But, as I told her in no-nonsense terms, I wanted her back when I reached Titan. And my father, also, must then make an appearance. I wanted them both to witness my final act of glory.

Now that I knew she had been sentenced to limbo, she was in no position to barter with these terms. She was promising me endless flame at Titan, but I knew I could not endure the desert with nothing to light, on my own. We were mutually dependent.

We walked together, back to the stone beach, and picked up the Zephyr. The boot was still loaded up with kerosene. We drove for two hours until we hit the next town. We bought both the available newspapers and a copy of Raymond B.Cowles' *Desert Journal* from the bookstore, so that we would have a guide in times of trouble. None of my acts of arson had hit the papers, so I was feeling a bit low. Momma held Titan out before me like the promise of ambrosia after a meal of Brussels sprouts. Even if nothing else made the news, then Titan surely would, and the other fires would then be reported on. It wasn't that I hadn't done good work; it was just that the Pterons and the cattery weren't buildings that anybody actually cared about. Once the desert was over, there would be a couple more Pterons and then the Big One, Titan. Ma suggested that I write the family name, rather than the name of the victim we had wreaked vengeance upon, and I agreed. I should have been writing 'nothing' all along. I had known that Mum would be full of good ideas.

By this stage, we were getting on pretty well. She'd changed out of her muddied green dress and into a pair of my old jeans and a leather jacket. For someone over forty, she looked pretty good. Now that she'd calmed down a bit, I was real proud to have her in the seat beside me. She was far better company than Lydia had ever been. We chatted happily for another hour, and then we hit the edge of the desert.

There was nothing as far as the eye could see; and silence as far as the ear could listen. Ma and I got out of the Zephyr and looked. We had not hit the sandy regions yet, and were standing on hard baked orange clay. Cracks shot out beneath our feet. I would like to say that there were buzzards circling overhead, but there weren't. There was only me and her and a terrifying silence.

"They say the first part's the worst part", said Ma, but I wasn't sure who 'they' were, nor when or how she'd been talking to them.

The sun was relentless. We were both drenched in sweat and my blood ran hot through my veins. As in all other times of adversity, I began to sing. Things were not so bad. I had a lot to look forward to. First of all, the torchable towns on the other side of the desert. Secondly, lighting the city of Titan. Thirdly, the exciting desert wildlife. I was hoping to see a lot of snakes. Snakes were beautiful creatures and people were stupid to be scared of them. They'd had a lot of bad press over the years; none of it deserved. I had read in a book about a snake professor who would move his hand rapidly towards the head of a very deadly snake. The snake would recoil in horror, lowering its head, submissively. It was the same when snakes were charged by lab rats. They never struck. They were really very shy, and probably had a thing about being looked at by all those eager first-year students. Once the professor had stuck two rats in a cage with a snake, and the next morning, found the snake looking depressed on the floor of the cage, and one of the rats sitting on top of the reptile, chewing its tail; a rare breakfast treat. Rattlesnakes, especially, seem to have got themselves a very bad rep. The general feeling seems to be; if you hear the rattle, you're down. This is ridiculous. The rattler is rattling to scare you away, so it doesn't have to resort to biting you for encroaching on its personal space. If it was really out to kill, it wouldn't rattle at all, but would slither up silently, and strike. I guess what I'm trying to say is that I feel pretty angry that human evil gets projected onto a beautiful and largely innocent creature. More people die by wasp stings than by snake bites, yet it is the nice snake that is seen as the summation of evil. Genesis has a lot to answer for, I think, and also human ignorance. I was really looking forward to seeing a few good reptiles. Apart from the ones in books, the only snakes I had ever seen had been in a snake-pit at the zoo at Enderby. Ma had taken me when I was about twelve, and I had been in love ever since. I doubted there would be any snakes here, at the edge of the desert, but as we got further in, I expected to make some friends. Ma would kill for a snake-skin handbag, I just knew it. Come to think of it, I wouldn't look half-bad in a pair of snaky trousers. I was a pretty skinny bastard, so a couple of meaty reptiles should do it. God! Pteron receptionists would be green with envy.

After thinking for five minutes about snakes and wearing them, I was feeling all warm and glowing inside. Ma had walked five hundred metres from the Zephyr, and was standing looking in towards the dead heart of the desert. I felt pretty heroic. This is the kind of thing you had to go through if you wanted to burn a big place like Titan. I was living my very own Boys Own Adventure. Also, just because we were in the desert, didn't mean there wasn't scope for burning. Momma was pointing to some banqueters who had set up shop not so far from where she stood, the legs of their table straddling some very large fissures in the earth. Oh God! The diners of my anaesthetic nightmares. To see them in the bright light of reality like this made me sick with terror. Silently, I motioned to Ma that she should get back into the car. I didn't know what they meant, but I knew that they were terrifying; an image of underground, surfacing. I guess Ma must've been kind of hungry, 'cause she started to walk towards them, a case of like attracting like. If she had not been already dead, I would have felt a little scared for her. Anyway, you know how it is, man's gotta think about number one in these kind of situations. Let the dead take care of their own. I jumped into the driver's seat of the Zephyr, stepped on the accelerator and left her there to sup. Who needs his Mother when he has his desert journal.

\*\*\*

It was the early morning hours and I was freezing my ass off on the back seat of the Zephyr. Something was bashing itself madly against the window.

"Piss off Ma", I yelled, but the thing kept up its banging. I switched on the interior light. It was a bat and a bloody great big one.

"Raymond?" I whimpered, knowing that the naturalist would not desert me in my most desperate hour. I could've handled the attempts of a snake to make its way inside, but a bat was too much of a burden to bear. I turned to the index. Bartholomew George, Bass white sea, Bat p.240.

*...any bat that seems overly familiar and flies about one in an unusual manner could be the victim of mental derangement because of rabies. One therefore should be cautious of bats that appear to be sick, weakened, or flying in an uncoordinated way.*

Oh God! I was going to die here, crazed and alone, having contracted rabies from a desert bat. This bat was definitely acting in a way that was 'overly familiar'. Bashing against panes was not normal Chiropteran behaviour. I looked to Raymond for further advice, but he'd changed the subject to porcupines and their dangerous shooting quills. The bulb in the indoor light popped and I was cast into darkness. Just my luck. Alone, in the dark, with an unseen enemy for whom night is its forte. Silence. Peace? No, it was back with a vengeance, back and flapping; great black wings. It had moved round to the front of the vehicle and was smacking itself into the windscreen. I thought I caught a glimpse of vampire fangs, and became scared that it would bite its way through the glass.

I fumbled in my pocket for the car keys and started up the engine. Still the bugger bashed. I shot forward, but, looking back, I could see I was being followed by a large black shadow. Christ! I felt a strange sort of admiration for a creature blessed with such determination. Still, I would show that bastard a match. I pulled over again, but left the headlights and the interior light on.

The bat was beating against the rear window pane. I reached over into the back seat and grabbed a half-empty tin of kerosene and the yellow lighter. I'll teach you to mess with King Of Fire, little bat. Stepping outside, I felt the bugger flying straight at my face. Like a prized matador, I moved neatly to one side, and saw the bat, unable to change it's course, flap on past. Then it swung or hovered, and I splashed a liberal dosage of kerosene up and over the big black beast. This, of course, seemed to anger it further, and, with a fury seemingly out of this world, it gathered force and dived. Simultaneously, I held up the lighter to the bat's underbelly. Remorse ran through me that I must destroy such a beautiful creature, but knowing that it was me or him, I pushed emotion from my mind. Flame spread up along the belly of the bat and out across his wingspan. The bulb of the Zephyr's interior light popped with a bang. Tears were welling up in my eyes. What grotesque acts of vivisection had I committed? Cats were one thing, but this gorgeous creature of the night was another. The bat paused for a moment, and peered down at me, as if to say, *Well? Happy now that I'm destroyed?* I shook my head in reply and started back towards the car in order to get some water to extinguish the flame I had created. But by then the bat had risen, and was flapping off slowly across the desert sky, both wings dripping brilliant orange flame. From where I stood I could see only the steady movement of the fire, up and down and up and down and then I started to remember and to cry.

## EPISODE THIRTEEN

### Break

My mother's breakdown had been an event completely beyond my father's level of comprehension. Breaking was something that happened to small juicy tree-twigs, prompting sap to ooze from the stalk. Breaking down was what happened to motor vehicles, inconveniently. When Ma finally lost it, in my last year of high school, the year that I turned eighteen, the thing that most put Dad out was the inconvenience factor of it all. He could take the yelling and plate smashing and the daytime TV viewing. What he found particularly hard to handle was the lack of meals prepared on time, the absence of clean underwear, the dust piling up on the furniture.

All the rules that Mother had previously driven by, she forgot. If she saw a red light, she stepped on the accelerator. If somebody said 'straight ahead' at a roundabout, she careered up and over the traffic island. Had she not lived her life appropriately up till now? Following all the rules. Marrying an electrician, having a child, raising a child. And then, nothing, no instructions, no rulebook to provide guidance. What was she meant to do with her days? She found the answer at the bottom of her empty vodka bottle, the one that was so frequently smashed against the wall in a grotesque parody of the Russian custom.

Dad and I ignored the whole thing to the best of our ability.

Ma was in Shackleton State Hospital for two long years, during which space of time I took on the role of housewife while Dad continued to work as an electrician. I finished my final year at high school, but did not attempt to find paid employment, as I knew I would be too busy performing all the tasks my mother had found were not enough to fill her life. Every day I vacuumed and dusted, beat the rugs on the outside porch, did all the washing and prepared meals for my father. This was all before I started the chef's course (at which I lasted four days) so my meals were the simple fare that one finds in small-town tearooms; re-heated sausage rolls, canned asparagus rolls with extra butter, crunchy lemon muffins. I knew that I could not cook to save myself, so every day at five p.m. I would run down to Norma's Tearooms and buy up anything Norma had not sold that day. I would remove the crusting brown wrapper from the sausage rolls, pop them in the oven and hope for the best. I would grease up an asparagus roll with another chunk of butter and slip that in beside the sausage roll. As long as it was soaked in sufficient grease, my father remained oblivious to whatever it was I served, chewing slowly and methodically and refusing to taste anything. If it had been a bad day at the tearooms, then my father and I would eat well that night, and, occasionally, we would have leftovers, so that the next day I would be spared a trip down the road. I would fry up a couple of the previous day's asparagus rolls in a bit of old lard and my father and I would sup like kings. We lived off Norma's Tearooms for the entire duration of the time that my mother was ill. I had once attempted to take Norma herself on a date to the movies, but before we even got to the door, she'd thrown up on the pavement outside the theatre, because she'd caught salmonella from a piece of undercooked chicken. From then on, I made a rule never to mix friendship with business. Given my absence of friends, this was remarkably easy. All in all, I stayed away from other people in order to allow myself time to keep the household running smoothly, and to keep up with a few extra-curricular activities.

Of course, I was always aware of the space within myself which arson would rush in to fill. Upon graduation, I found that just as housework had not been enough for my mother, so it was not enough for me, yet I did not have enough spare time to take a job. So instead I resorted to taking up a hobby; butterfly collecting.

On the wall above my bed I pinned a board on which to mount the specimens I had captured. I dedicated my mornings to catching and etherising monarchs and whites, my afternoons to housekeeping and my nights to getting the critters prepared and arranged. The routine went as follows. The minute I heard my father's car choking out of the garage, I would leave the dishes that I was washing, and run upstairs to get my net. Two blocks over from our house were a series of large vacant paddocks frequented by both monarchs and white cabbage butterflies, the only two critters I ever caught. (Lack of variety in my collection did not bother me; I exhibited for an appreciative audience of one.) I took to the paddock a small selection of glass jars within which to keep the flies whilst on fieldwork. The jars intended for monarchs I marked with a small maroon spot, and I placed a white star on the side of those meant for the white cabbage flies. My hobby was an exercise in patience. I would crouch in the long grass, one hand on my net, wrapping my parka about my torso, keeping warm, and trying to ignore the stiffening muscles in my legs. Then I would feel it; the familiar flittering about my face, the beating of small white wings. (Presuming it was a cabbage. Small maroon and brown wings, if it was a monarch.) A shock of adrenalin, not unlike that I would later experience when lighting, would shoot through me. But then was not the time to pounce. I would hold my breath, (difficult because I had been a chain smoker since age eleven), and wait for the flittering to change to fluttering and for the fluttering to settle. And when the air ceased to tremble around those tiny wings, I would slam down my net and catch the bugger between the mesh and the ground. I loved the panic and the increase in the rate at which the wings beat. I relished the fact that I had caught something which once had flown, and now would sit, outstretched upon my wall.

I would hold my jar up to the net, slide my prisoner into the appropriate glass jar and slam on the lid. This was the most difficult part; the stage at which the captured was most likely to make its escape. I had torn many perfectly good specimens simply through jamming the lid on too early and catching the wing as I screwed the top on tight. Once the butterfly was in the jar, he'd really said his last goodbye.

I usually caught six or seven at a time, all in individual jars, and labelled them as either cabbage or monarch. Then I'd throw the whole lot into a day-tripper pack I owned, walk the short distance home, take my bounty upstairs to my room and prepare for the next stage of the operation. This following part was comparatively easy. I had purchased a large aquarium especially for the purpose of etherising. I would slide across the piece of Perspex with which I covered the tank and release the butterflies into the tank for a last little fly around, as I slid the cover back over. On top of my dresser

I kept a wad of cotton wool and a little bottle of ether which I had nicked from the Chemistry lab at school. Taking one last glance at the day's catch, I would pour ether onto a hunk of the cotton and shove it in with the butterflies, watching their wing beats slow and eventually cease.

I found this to be a most enjoyable way to pass my mornings. As for the rest of the day, well, as previously explained, I would play at housewife until Pa came home for that evening's meal, courtesy of Norma. After I had washed all the dishes, I would run back up the stairs to my room and continue on from where I had left off. I have always had an obsessive streak.

Picking the corpses up from out of the tank, I would carefully pin them, through the bodies, to my special mounting board, a satisfaction in work well done that was not matched until the day I torched my first Pteron. These were the activities my life consisted of until that day when Ma made it out of the hospital; in one piece, now, having been shattered like a porcelain plate and glued back together. My own life collapsed when my parents decided to pay for a housekeeper so that I might find full-time employment. Employment was the last thing I wanted. Of course, you will remember, that I had not yet discovered my true calling and so, although I carried within me the emptiness which fuels all acts of destruction, I had not yet discovered how to utilize the potential which such vacuousness represented. I had failed all my science papers, so a career in entomology was out of the question, as was an escape to Enderby University. I might have been eligible to apply for special entry into a music course, given my outstanding grades in this one field, but further education did not interest me. Not a lot did. My grades, (D's in Science and Maths, C's in English and, the one saviour, my A's in music), were not due to lack of ability, but general lack of enthusiasm. Nothing was quite so boring as school. I never did any of the work that was set for me, and, when required to sit tests, would give the wrong answers on purpose.

Also, I was myopic, but too vain to wear glasses, so most of my school life passed in a blur of mis-read words. This was the way I liked it. Why should I bring my life into sharp focus? Things were easier to handle when they were smudged and misinterpreted. My parents were too preoccupied with their own lives to pay any attention to report cards.

Music lessons were the only part of school I approached with any sense of desire. No matter how hard I tried, I just couldn't seem to stuff it up. The teacher would play a tune, slowly, on the piano, and I would hear the name of each note, being spoken, loud in my ear. And should I try to write down something which was not been spoken to me, I would suffer a piercing migraine, and have to leave the classroom to eat six Panadol. So it was not through any ability or effort of my own that I achieved my excellent music grades. It was just that I had no choice. And perhaps I should have pursued a career as a musician. But the simple fact of the matter was, I could afford no instrument, and, besides which, I was too ugly. I lost interest in my butterfly collection.

And so it was that I took up walking. I walked and I walked and I walked. My parents assumed that I was out searching for jobs. After a month or so of walking, I didn't find a job (I hadn't been looking), but I did find my own place to live; a scungy one bedroom flat as far from my parents home as it was possible to get in a town with a population of five thousand. So, for two long years, I was a professional stroller. The sense of purpose in my stride would have been enough to make any onlooker assume that I had a set destination. And I did: Destination Nowhere. Past the cafe, past the library, past the museum, time and time and time again. I had muscles in places where no muscles were meant to be. And then I found the chef's course, and the nature of flame and addiction.

## *Noon*

Because I had slept too long in the sun, my skin was pink, raw and itching. I had fallen asleep with my head against the car window; a window which was now streaky with last night's tears. It was midday. The sun was high and burnt with an absolute ferocity. Crying over a bat; what a bloody sook. Things were getting dangerous; Ma had deserted me for a bunch of banqueters, the interior light of my car was stuffed, I was sleeping excessively, the sun was burning white-hot and I was upsetting myself over dead animals. For God's sakes! I had been destroying animals for the best part of ten years, I should not be getting upset about it now. And yet, I was. The realisation of what I had become dawned upon me, as harsh as the overhead sun.

A wet blanket, that's what I had turned into. A bloody great girl's blouse. If I did not pull myself together quick-smart I would be a skeleton within no time at all; left out here as carrion for the vultures which were now circling the skies above. Dead meat. I started up the engine.

A tap at the window startled me. It was my father, assuming human form. I could hardly contain my joy. He motioned for me to wind down the window.

"What the hell've ya done with ya mother?"

"She was hungry."

"You mean to say you've gone and lost her?"

The dead have no sense of tact. I revved the engine impatiently.

"She's just gone for a bit of dinner with some old friends."

"Who?"

Also, no sense of privacy.

"Just some guys on the edge of the desert."

"You irresponsible little twit. I'm gonna do you for this one."

Also, no sense of mercy.

"Come on Dad. You never really liked her anyway."

"She was my wife! I loved her!"

Yea, yea, yea.

"What?"

"Nothing."

"You're not just going to go on without her are you?"

"She can catch up with me later. She always has in the past."

"But now you don't have a past. It's been erased."

"What?"

"You have no past, so what happened in it doesn't matter."

"You're missing the point Pa. The point is that I'm telling you not to worry. Ma'll catch up with me..."

"She'll catch her death, that's the only thing she'll be catching."

"She's already dead."

That stumped him. I revved the engine again. He tried for a comeback.

"What I mean is..."

"What you mean is, without me burning the Big One, you'll never make it through those pearly gates, and without Ma by my side, I'll never burn the Big One."

"I, also, am important in this piece of history."

"Yes, father, I'm sure you are."

*Never lifted a finger to help me in your entire life.*

"Pardon?"

"Nothing."

"It's me you'll be depending on in the heart of this nothing."

"Yes, Daddy, you shall be my desert oasis."

"That's right son. I shall be your well in times of drought."

Also, no sense of sarcasm.

"For a start, I've brought you this."

He handed me an oil lamp. I held it in my right hand.

"This is great Pa."

"Well you burst the interior light, didn't you?"

"That            was            the            bat's            fault."

"I don't care whose fault it was. You just take bloody good care of that lamp. It was mine, and it was my father's and his father's before him and so on and so forth."

He was just like Ma.  Always pulling the ancestry trip. "You hand me an oil lamp at midday. What foresight father, what goddamn foresight."

"It's something your mother always credited me with."

Only when she'd been drinking.

"WHAT?!"

"NOTHING!"

"Aren't you going to go back for her?"

"I can't turn back now Pa. It's getting late."

"We'll I'll go back then, since you've no sense of duty. That's the problem with you young ones. You do your best to bring them up decent, and whadda you get. No bloody thanks at all. They just take what you give them, and they're off."

Yep. I stepped on it, and me and the Zephyr shot forwards, deeper into the heart of nothing. Gripping the steering wheel between my knees and switching the lamp from my right hand to my left, I dexterously lit an empty cigarette box and threw it, flaming, from the car.

Goodbye my father, I thought.

I hold the light.

## *EPISODE FOURTEEN*

### *The Long Look Back*

When I look back now, I am never quite sure how I managed to chart those unmapped territories. Had I been lucky or had I just been cursed? There was no way of knowing anything: what was past and what was present, what was fact and what was fiction, what was true and what had all just been a big lie.

I suppose the whole experience had been what you might call 'character building'. I had, as they say, made something out of nothing.

I had made myself.

## *Motel Paradiso*

Everything was coming up roses. The sky itself was bursting with them: Silver Jubilee, Whisky Mac, Victor Borge, Remember Me. A canopy in tones of red; an overhead projection, singing and exploding.

    Ma and Pa were here beside me. I trusted they had enjoyed their time playing dinner guests. Pa's hand was pressed firmly on my shoulder, in a paternal 'that's my boy' gesture. I was my father's son. I knew he was trying to grease me up for Titan, but it did not matter. Not only was the sky roses, but the sides of the road were coated in luscious greenery; it was really quite a show. Titan was till a few days drive away, but between here and there I would not be bored. Ma had reassured me of the presence of a few Pterons, so that would be good sport. I had no memories bugging me neither; the ghosts of my past had strutted and fretted out their hours. Finally, I sensed the beginnings of peace. Peace, HA! that was a good one.

    The odd vehicle was passing in the opposite direction, but I did not pay much attention. It struck me that I was becoming something of a solipsist. The broken sign on the side of the road.

WELCOME TO CARNEY.
Another psychotic receptionist. Another cheesy Pteron.

***

I woke up alone and frozen to my bed. My eyes were on fire. I reached up to touch them and there was blood on my hands. Somebody had been lacerating me in the night. Probably that sneaky receptionist. I staggered to the mirror but I couldn't see anything. I put my hand down on the glass and felt it cold as ice. I moved to the window and felt the cold outside air. Something was damn fishy. I was sure I had fallen asleep in a nice ordinary Pteron, and here I was, awakening in an ice hotel with hacked-up eyes. It never ended. I called out for my Ma but there was nobody home and I was freezing.

The blood was beginning to clear and I could make my way to my trousers. They were frozen to the floor. Everything was made of ice; white and sparkling, dangerous and beautiful. My movements were slowing down. I was a fly caught in a deep-freeze. I pulled on my rigid trousers and sat down on the carved ice sofa. Bloody comfy. Pity the telly was dead. I called out for the Abyssinian mirror desert diners but nothing happened. The mirror began to crack. I walked over and peered at what should have been my own reflection but was only frozen glass and water.
One last friend to call on.
The tentative whimper went out.
"Dad?"
My eyes were still clouded with the blood but I thought I saw him appear momentarily in the ice. Then I reached up to rub my face and when I looked again, saw nothing. I wanted to see my father or myself so badly - any image of myself to know that I was still in existence. There was nothing in the mirror but the widening fissures and the frozen glass. My hands were made of ice. Everything was solid and glinting and clear.

The ghosts were strutting and fretting still. I couldn't believe they didn't know when to stop, it was getting ridiculous, this constant cattle prod in the back of my neck, constant lightening at the knees. I didn't ask for this! All I had ever wanted was a life as a nice normal arsonist, not all this shite and baggage that went along with it. I called again, dialling a dead line.
"Dad?"

There was no man to meet.

I was seeing through lines of blood where the cuts were healing. My toes were up against the wall I was praying for my father to help me and getting a teency bit scared but his face never appeared or crashed through the wall till I was moving through the mirror. My hair was full of glass and splints. There was a carving in the ice; a man. I saw myself; an image, a mannequin, a dumb ice doll. All your dreams will come true.

All my dreams have come true.

All vacancy, all heat.

# EPISODE FIFTEEN

*Whole.*

I was twenty years old when my Ma made it out of the hospital and twenty-two when I lit the farmhouse. If my mathematics do not let me down, this makes for a two year space of nothing happening. A very strange section of time; a spell in limbo, a period of complete mental frigidity. Oh, of course, I was very active physically. I walked, didn't I? Nobody could say that was rotting in my own juices. But it was as if only by keeping my limbs in motion could I convince myself that I was 'going somewhere'. In many ways, I was already gone, having been over the edge of that steepest precipice, holding tightly onto my mother's hand, two years previously. I knew that if I didn't light, I would be consumed by my own flame, yet for two years I did nothing. I found myself moving through spaces I had no comprehension of.

Everything slowed down and I found myself moving in between the different layers of time. The smallest second could open up to become a vacuous gap at any given opportunity. You had to be on guard constantly, you never knew when a simple tick was going to open up into a gaping chasm. I was like a kid on the monkey bars, blindfolded; swinging across from bar to bar, groping helplessly for the next rung. I did not see my Ma and Pa much 'cause they were having a few marital problems and Rose was in some prison or home somewhere whilst her Pa still drank and ranted and bashed the walls, so I suppose I did not see much of anybody worth seeing.

I was not walking a tightrope; I was walking a flimsy piece of cotton thread.

I could hear the voice of my father, telling me to make something of my life, but I couldn't make anything. I did not want to do some stupid music course at Enderby University; nobody was going to tell me how to write a tune, lest of all some dickhead professor. I didn't know how to play any instruments anyway, I just hummed the little tunes I had in my head, and occasionally beat time on a couple of old saucepans. Although it may sound as if limbo was an unpleasant place, I actually quite enjoyed it; well, I enjoyed the song bits anyway. I always trilled when I was walking, made up bass lines, stuff like that; a right regular little canary.

Every day was Sunday morning and Sunday morning was Judgement Day.

I did have a couple of friends; Ulric and Walt, two old blokes who lived down under the bridge which ran across Shackleton's main (only) river. Black as the Styx it was too. They'd tried to get me interested in the meths, since that was basically their chief form of sustenance, but I had never been too into that, I didn't see the point in it, nor substances or anything. You always paid out more than you got. I mean, if you had a high that went to five, then you had a low that went to negative seven. If you had a high that went to six you had a low that went to negative eight, and if you had a high that went to ten, God help you later, 'cause I couldn't. Me, I had enough problems dealing with my ricocheting moods without any help from external substances.

These guys were alright though; the only two decent people left in Shackleton since Rose had left. Damn good for conversation. They were right into their books; Ulric had experienced a full-on English education fifty years back and liked to quote Old Bill at me;

> *For I have sworn thee fair and thought thee bright*
> *Who are as black as hell as dark at night.*

He also fancied himself as a bit of a poet in his own right and would rant his 'songs for the tone deaf' in different voices; he was a great big mad man and usually dressed in an old maroon pinstriped suit that was most becoming. Ulric's poetry was all pretty shit but it was great entertainment, just because he made such a show of it and it was the only time me and Walt could get him into drag. His costumes had to be nicked from the Larger Ladies store on the main street, and were all real classy. He did Lady Macbeth like nothing you've ever seen; hot pink lycra, belly hanging out the front, desperately clutching a bottle of meths in one hot hand.

**Lady Macbeth Kills King Duncan Even Though He Looks Like Her Father. She is Caught by Interrogators.**

O you can't prove anything.

Did you see me do it?

I never thrust that cutting edge into his chest
and I never watched in astonishment
as his torso collapsed
and fell open to reveal
that revolting sack of ribs.

On those wrecked bones hung all the letters of the alphabet.

Just like gutting a fish.

Makes a girl quite ill to think of it.

But you can't prove anything.

For all you know
I may have been out slaughtering sheep
or assisting in the delivery
of my servant's baby.

I never wiped the dagger clean
or did I never wash it?

(pause)

What do you mean obsessive-compulsive?

(pause)

I never stabbed and stabbed and stabbed and stabbed and stabbed.

What do you think I am?  A psychopath?

(pause)

It was a rhetorical question.

(pause)

No.
It was the guards.
The two of them.
I saw them with my own eyes
they were
so savage
and so brutal.

I can't remember after that.

O, I feel faint!

Could I have a glass of water, please?

Anyway,
How do you think it was for me
stuck away in that crumbly old palace
while you were off fighting
in your wars and what-not.

Day after day, night after night,
rattling around in all those empty rooms
staring at the portraits of my
husband's ancestors
which hung on the wall
behind the stairwell.
Time on my hands.

And all those ridiculous ladies-in-waiting.

The murder?

I kept on looking.
I couldn't help myself.

Still, you can't prove anything.

What happened is between
Duncan, the guards and I.

Well the old man's dead,
the guards are silent,
and I am guilty of nothing.

He'd pause, take a bow, and Walt and I would applaud and cheer, thanking God that no-one else could see, and praying Ulric would chose not to inflict another one on us that day.

The second bloke, Walt, was about half Ulric's size and even weedier than I was, a true rodent of a man, uncannily reminding me of the rats I had shared such happy times with several years previously. While Ulric ranted, Walt would sort of hum along in the background; an accompaniment.

It was nice the way they helped each other out and all that. If one of them got the shakes the other one would be right there with condolences and various sensible words of advice, each needing the other like a crutch, there was no doubting it. They were a married couple, really, and their relationship was a damn sight better than my parents' had ever been.

They would've been RSA buddies if they'd gone to war, but Ulric had been a conscientious objector and Walt hadn't been admitted due to eczema, asthma, hay fever and a nasty psychiatric history that made Charles Manson look as harmless as the proverbial lamb.

They were both pretty anxious that I know one was not buggering the other.

"We're just chums, son, that's all there is to it", Ulric would say, reaching over to pinch Walt's left buttock.

"OW! Girlfriend!" Walt would squeal.

And giggle and knock back a bit more meths.

After all the rednecks I'd had to put up with elsewhere, they were just such damn good company. Walt would dress up in some glam outfit he'd got from a clothing bin and parade round in the mud on the edge of the river.

"Straight as a crochet needle", he'd protest, waggling a painted fingernail at me.

They would've been able to rent a place if they didn't drink their entire pension, but I don't think they were that interested in having a home anyway. They'd made themselves a lovely little bed from some old bits of driftwood tied together with string and strategically placed it beneath a concrete overhang. It really was paradise, especially when it snowed. I don't think that many other people could have lived this way, but I suppose that when you've got your meths you've got a firm and loving friend. They drank to get away from the sun, they drank to get away from the snow, they drank to get away from everything, even, I think, each other.

They thought I was pretty soft, just being on the dole and living by myself and not really doing much of anything. I told them I was finding my feet, and they said I should try looking on the end of my legs, before I got old and legless. They were pretty funny.

When Ma got out of Shackleton State Hospital, I used to go visit them every day. They tried to get me interested in my life and would suggest various possible career paths. Ulric was all for me taking to the street and busking and Walt was all for me taking to the street and selling myself, as he had done, in Titan, when he was younger. Ulric was sure I could earn a packet spouting his poetry on the streets of Titan. I tried to assure him that this was not the case, but he insisted that there was money to be made. I had no desire to humiliate myself on the streets of the city I had grown up in, and attempted to impress this upon him but he would not listen. He was an arrogant bastard, underneath that camp exterior. When you got him going there was no stopping him. You'd hear some little sentence starting off and you knew it was going to become a torrential outpouring. Scared the pants. He couldn't do anything straight; he needed alcohol like most people need air. It was only drunk that he could pull himself together and function properly.

It was nice to be under the bridge with them, away from my grotty little flat; like belonging to some repertory theatre group with only two members. That was where my time was spent when I wasn't walking; it was better to hang with Walt and Ulric during the day and walk at night than vice versa. I'd only been to see them once after dark, and it was like hell down there; wet and cold with the cars zooming overhead the only noise that cut the night. During the day you could kid yourself that they wanted to live that way; at night it became dead obvious that they had no choice, that they'd drunken themselves into a corner and there was no getting out.

## Drive

We were driving again, the three of us, on one side of the mirror or the other. The sign on the side of the road still said Highway Naught. Ma was saying sorry about the hotel freezing over, she hadn't foreseen it and I was yea yea yea too late, keep your apologies I've lived through it now all in the past. Dad was sleeping in the back seat, occasionally waking up to check the map, then lying back down, his head jarred against the door. I'd smoked all the Marlboroughs and was getting a bit titchy, short nerves and all that. I was beginning to wonder whether Titan wasn't a figment of my imagination, too long spent with nothing but the dead for company. But it was, in Ulric's own words, the O so shining city, a silver dot on a map of whiteness. I hadn't come so far out or up or in just to be locked out as Ulric had. The only way in to the city was to torch it and that had long been my plan. I had to keep going though I couldn't. High school with no recess.

## Split

One day I went down underneath the bridge and they had gone. I called and called but nobody answered me. I waded in amongst the bulrushes and muddy waters at the side of the river, half expectant of a baby in a basket. The heads lay side by side in the shallow water; two papier mâché balloons. Cold and silent and still; the pale faces of bloated fish.

That was the first night I lit.

The rest, as they say, is history.

# EPISODE SIXTEEN

*On*

I never knew whether Ulric and Walt had been the instigators of their own deaths. I guess I didn't care.

I didn't care about anything.

We stopped at a Mobil for some Marlboroughs which I then chain smoked for the next hour and a quarter while Ma cheered me on in my acts of cell destruction. What did lung cancer matter; we had a city to torch and were destined to die in the flames anyway. Besides, cigarettes are good for you.

I did what I always do when I feel emotive; I hummed, reflecting on what a great bloke I was and surely destined for the great gold city; holiest of holies. I'd look fab in those white flowing robes; pair of plastic wings stuck on my shoulder blades and a paper plate for a halo.

Ma divined my thoughts.
"You know you can't wear white, you'll spill your dinner on it."
For Petes sakes.
"It's my fantasy Mother, I'm the one in charge."
"Don't kid yourself little boy. You're just the pawn in your mother's movie."
Like I said, no mercy.
"Well I'm none too fond of the script."
"Lucky it's about to end then, eh boyo?"
That really scared me. I'd had too much too soon, way too much. Though I hadn't asked for anything. What would I have after Titan? If Saint Pete condescended to let me through the gates, what would I do all day in heaven? Sit round and play a harp? That would be boring. It struck me that the whole arson thing had become slightly out of control.

A far worse thought was Pete hitting down button on the elevator. Images of myself endlessly rowing across a burning lake of fire flashed before my eyes. At least it would be exciting and it couldn't be very much worse than my life had been so far. I could still feel the freezer burns on my arms from the ice hotel.

"That's what you get when you don't stick to your Pterons", said Ma helpfully.

"How was I meant to know it wasn't a Pteron? It had the giant 'P' outside."

"Pteron's 'P's are white", said Ma, "that one was purple and stood for Paradiso."

I lit another cigarette.

"Where are we staying tonight then?"

"You'll have to wake your father up. He's the one with the map."

"Pa?"

No reply.

"Pa?"

Nothing.

"PA!"

He bolted upright, hitting his head on the car ceiling. Useless git.

"What's the next town?"

He groped for the map.

"Balleny."

"Is there a 'P' next to it on the map?"

He squinted.

"Yea."

"Purple or white?"

"Purple."

Damn.

"Where's the next white 'P', Pa?"

He scanned again. Ma tapped her fingers impatiently on the dashboard.

"Rothschild. There's a white 'P' at Rothschild."

"How far?"

"About three centimetres."

"Ma! Can you take the map off him?"

She reached across to the back seat.

"Give it to me, dear."

He obliged, snuffled and returned to sleep.

"It's a couple of hours drive away", said Ma.

The road was nice; none of the earlier excess of rose, but some good greenery. Ma and I played Eye Spy and I got her for an hour and a half with "blur". She took a turn at driving. I sat in the passenger's seat and tried not to think. It was important for me to retain focus. I had set my goal (Titan) and must achieve it. Whatever came after that, it would be out of my hands. Of course, there would be a couple of Pterons on the way for sport, but these could not be taken seriously.

I switched on the car radio. Crackling static. I switched off the car radio.

Ma and I exchanged places. I wondered how much kerosene we had left.

"Enough", said Ma.

So there was nothing for me to think about and I was left alone with vacancy until we reached Rothschild.

ROTHSCHILD PTERON

Same old, same old. More purple vinyl more hard green plastic.

I fell asleep with a cigarette still burning in the corner of my mouth.

***

When I woke up I was on the floor and they were laying into me with hard steel boots.

CRACK!

Was that a rib?

"YOU STUPID FUCK!"

I did not know what I had done.

"It's all thanks to you!"

What crime I had commited.

"Momma?"

"YOU LITTLE SHIT!"

Or failed to commit.

"He's no son of mine. I want a divorce."

Dad was somewhere up near my head. I felt the boot hit home.

"HOI! Take it easy!"

And other effectual words.

"YOU LEFT THE KEYS IN THE IGNITION BOY!"

"Whoops."

"Whoops is right. Do you know the effort I had to go to in order to get that Zephyr?"

"Yes Momma."

"By God I knew I should've hedged my bets and had more than one child."

"Yes Momma."

"Changed the licence plates and everything."

"Yes Momma."

Just please stop kicking my ribs in.

"I'll steal another one for you Ma, I promise."

"Oh it's no good now. Steal one from a place as small as Rothschild and the coppers'll be onto you in two seconds flat. Enderby was a nice big city with lots of vehicles to nick. There's only two people in this town and they both own this motel."

An exaggeration. I hated it when she did that. Rothschild didn't just have a motel; it had a pub and a petrol station as well.

She turned some of her wrath upon Pa.

"Well don't just stand there with your mouth hanging open. The flies'll get in. Go on and get the map from the car. See how far we've got to go."

No Poppa, please, don't leave me alone with this madwoman.

"I tell you what boy, you're gonna find it bloody hard to hitch a lift looking like that. Damned mess. Go and clean yourself up a bit."

Yes Momma.

I crawled off to the bathroom. The mirror was glass not ice and I could see myself clearly. I was bruised, not bleeding. I looked alright. Dunno what Ma was bloody talking about. At least I was human. I wiped over my face with a damp cloth and smoothed my hair with spit. Pretty hot news, damn straight. I smiled and waved at my nothingness in the mirror. Alright. Back in the main room,

Pa had brought the map in from the car and was spreading it out on the sofa. This sole act required his full concentration.

"Ten centimetres", he said.

Six or seven hours driving then, which could translate into any number of days hitching. Ma faced me.

"Well I'm not hitching with you if that's all you can do to make yourself tidy. Bloody pathetic."

She was unbearable when she got on her high horse. Real snobby cow.

Pa wasn't much to look at these days, neither, and Ma soon picked up on this.

"And you're not much better, lousy excuse for a husband."

She was reverting to the old pre-Shackleton patterns.

"Snap out of it Ma, you can't abuse us like you used to."

That went down terribly.

"If it wasn't for me you'd still be in jail."

She had a point. My father and I were both pretty useless and on top of that, ugly. We couldn't torch the Pteron due to lack of a getaway car.

She hitched out of Rothschild before us. Each of us had a pack. It took her an hour and a quarter to get picked up, 'cause me and my father were timing. Then we went out after her and stood, thumbs out, waiting, and me singing to pass the time.

> *Remember when the scenery started fading*
> *I held you till you learned to walk on air*
> *So don't look down, the ground is gone*
> *There's no-one waving, anyway*
> *The smoky life is practised everywhere*

The rain beat down. In a pack, we carried the gasoline. It took us a while to get a lift.

## *Hands*

Did history ever happen?

I think I remember finding Walt and Ulric, drowned by accident or intention, but I can never really be sure.

I couldn't be sure of anything 'cause history was a big lie.

I had nothing on my hands.

Not history, nor time, nor blood.

*When you've got nothing you've got nothing to lose.*

## Slide

One more mess on the side of the road. One more carrion, carnage, wrecked old hag. She never should've chosen to assume human form, she always should've stayed in limbo. Once you're human, you're vulnerable.

Lesson learnt: stay dead.

Right then and there, on the side of the road, I got down in the gravel and prayed to Saint Pete to let Ma into heaven. Oh, I knew I'd whinged about her and she'd been a nag and all that, but didn't want her to burn eternally; hell, no.

*Let her in Saint Pete, let her in.*

We had no coffin for her body parts.

She'd been fairly well hacked. Psychos all over these highways. Just let them try something on me and Pa, I'd show them what for. We piled her into Pa's backpack.

*Sorry Ma. I never thought it would end like this.*

It was a little grotesque.

*We'll get there Ma, we'll get there.*

We were an hour or two past Rothschild. The guy who'd dropped us off when we'd started yelling at the sight of Ma's body had careered off into the distance and who could blame him. Not I, not I...

*Not I.*

*Shut up Ma, you're dead. Lie down.*

Silence.

We waited another hour or so in the hammering rain and were picked up by a nice man whose chest hair grew into his beard. He was a very eager beaver.
"Howdy howdy where ya off to in this dreadful weather?"
"Titan."
It had been decided that I would do the talking. Pa was a little shaken up at the death of his wife.
"Take ya halfway then. Hop on in folks. Packs in the boot."
Pa shot me a quivering look. We disobeyed and slid the pack into the back seat, between us. He didn't seem to care.
"What you got in the bag fellas. Human body? Ha heh ha heh ha heh."
Donkey bray.
"Just a few possums", I said - damned quick thinking.
"Been hunting eh?"
No we found them in a heap on the side of the road you stupid idiot.
"Ah, yes."
"I was quite into hunting myself once."
Lord preserve us, here we go.
"Bit of a man about the bush if I do say so myself."
Good-O.
"Till I went a bit funny and shot the old wife. Then I had to take it easy for a bit."
Holy hell.
"Not into that firearm business anymore."
Thank God.
"You're a quiet bloke. Long day out with the critters?"
"Uh-huh."
Don't encourage conversation. Stay calm.
Quietly, Pa was weeping. Driver didn't notice. Ma's hand was falling out the top of the pack, palm upwards. She had a very cracked lifeline.
"Nobody ever suspected me."
No, I don't suppose they would.
"She's was screwing my best buddy."

Oh, bloody asking for it mate.

"I was supposed to be on a hunting trip out of town. Came back and put a bullet through the head."

Pity it wasn't your own. I pushed Ma's hand back into the pack.

*Stay dead old girl, stay dead.*

Looking out the back window I could see three mad buzzards flapping after us, hanging in the sky; great black shadows of doom. We were cutting through cliff country. Eager beaver was still gabbling. I had to put a stop to this.

"Listen mate. We only wanted a lift. We did not want you to talk our ears off. Do you hear what I'm saying?"

I was not scared of psychos. I had the dead on my side.

"You getting cheeky with me young man?"

Within the pack, Pa was caressing Ma's hand and whimpering.

"Na, I am not getting cheeky. I just want a bit of peace, do you hear me? A bit of peace."

I knew that he'd either shut the hell up or kick us out of the car. Either way, I could not stand his bloody gabbling for one minute more. It was driving me insane. That's the trouble with these drivers who pick up hitchhikers. They want something back for their bother; they want your ear so they can talk it off. What they want is a shoulder to cry on, a post to lean on, and the fact that you're a total stranger makes it all the more enticing to them. He responded favourably.

"Well you only needed to say, didn't you? I didn't realise my speaking was such a burden."

It was pretty funny when someone you didn't even know tried to pull a guilt trip on you. That's really cracked me up.

"Suppose you're gonna toss one of those possums my way then, are you? Been missing them since I had to give up my hunting."

Pa yelped.

"Oh no, not these possums", I said. "These ones are special things we went to a very lot of trouble to get. We do not want to go on and give them away. We just want to keep them for ourselves."

He grunted. This was better than speech. Most things were better than speech. At least he hadn't booted us out of the car.

My hands were beginning to itch. I had to light something soon or I was going to be in big trouble. I could feel the tension building up somewhere near my temples. I fumbled in my pocket for a light.

I lit a cigarette.

The sight of the flame brought back all the old emotions; the hunger, the waiting, the expectation of exhilaration. I looked over at Pa. He had curled up around the pack which contained his wife. Out the rear window, the buzzards still flapped. I burnt a small lock of my own hair.
"JESUS!"
Beaver stepped on the brake.
Ahead of us was collapse. The rains had brought the river up and a good many logs had come playfully downstream and smashed up the bridge. It was a bit of a mess. I pulled Pa out of the car and onto the roadside. He was in no state to be witnessing such devastation, but I did not want him to be staying in that psycho's car a moment longer. He pulled Ma out after him and I fossicked in the pack for the kerosene.

*Let the punishment fit the crime.*

Of course, it was never my fault that he burnt. It was his own, for shooting his wife. It was on her behalf I was avenging, it was never on my own. I did not derive any satisfaction from it; I was only acting as Justice's servant.

*Please, believe me.*

There was a dreadful stench, worse than the cats, and Pa and I were stuck on the wrong side of the river, no way to get across and a dead mother in a backpack. I turned to my father.
"We can't take the old girl", I said. "She's too heavy. We'll have to leave her here."
He began to blubber, oblivious to the fact that I had just lit a man; too trapped in his own interior world of pain and suffering.

"It's what she would have wanted", he said. "She would've wanted to see you burn the city."
"We're not even going to reach the city at this stage."
He had not liked her that much when he was alive. He only wanted her now that she was gone.
"There'll be plenty of other women up at Titan, Pa. Like they say, plenty of fish in the sea."
"But I don't want another fish. I want this one."
It was pretty pathetic.
I looked over at Eager Beaver's barbequed body and whispered to myself a few small words of congratulation. Nice work. Some people deserve to die.

Justice is served.

The river was raging up about our waists. Pa had his wife on his back; her blood was washing out into the water, it was none too pleasant. I tried not to think about anything except the torrent we were crossing, but thoughts of Eager Beaver kept weaving their way back into my mind. I couldn't believe he'd actually killed his wife. For all I knew he was probably the one who'd reduced Ma to the state we'd found her in. The world was not a very nice place. Looking over at Pa, struggling across the river with my mother in a backpack, I felt a warm glow spread through me. It was good to know there were people in the world who knew how to stick to their values.

The absence of Ma's spirit meant she had finally found some resting place. This was why I was not upset. I knew Pa hadn't realised this, but it's not one of those things you can tell people. They either know it or they don't. Ma would be looking on now, and smiling, and hoping we'd make it to the city.

Then I was under the water.

***

My mother was floating past me in pieces. She looked better dismembered than she had whole, the water bearing her gracefully downstream, those segments and fractions of a person. The head went past, the hair billowing out the back like the sails of a yacht, the eyes wide open like two blind pearls.

I never looked down.

Before me was the city and the blaze began.

It was the city and I was there. The light stretched out in all directions as far as your eye could see. Pa was holding onto my hand and weeping. It was all damned beautiful. All my dreams; vengeance with a capital V. I was clutching my kerosene in one hot hand and my lighter in the other; what more could you ask for from a finale. Nothing; it's everything you've ever wanted.

I was mildly euphoric. This was the end of what had started when I was squeezed out from between my mother's thighs this was my way to get back back back and here I was, arsenal in hand. I'd been to hell for this, fifty thousand million times and here was I, about to get my just desserts. It was a pity Ma was not here to see my final culminant act of destruction, but I was sure that she herself had found a happy home.

What I hope that I have told you about is how it all began and how I could never be sure whether I was sliding or on the ascent but how it was the same thing anyway.

With my father by my side, I lit ninety-five buildings that night. And, looking back over my shoulder, I couldn't see nothing, but orange light and flickering flame as all the city burned.

And my nothing self dissolving into empty air and light.

## *Acknowledgments -*

*Life In The Desert.* Produced by Robert Raymond, Opus Films, Australia.
Desert Journal. Raymond B.Cowles, University of California Press, 1977, California.

p.137.
*Goodbye my father, I thought. I hold the light.*
Throwing Muses. Dizzy. From Hunkapapa. (4AD, 1989)

This Smoky Life Leonard Cohen, Recent Songs (Columbia, 1979)

www.ingramcontent.com/pod-product-compliance
Lightning Source LLC
Chambersburg PA
CBHW030536130626
46552CB00006B/2277